ACE OF MAIDS

THE ELITE MULTI-AUTHOR SERIES

THE ELITE
BOOK 3

K. L. HIERS

Ace of Maids

Hiers, K.L.

Proofread and Edited by Jennifer Griffin of Marked and Read

Formatted by Delaney Rain Author Services

Spade by Dolly Holmes & decorative swirl by ME from Noun Project

Cover Art © Morningstar Ashley Designs

Cover content is for illustrative purposes only and any person depicted is a model.

CHAPTER 1

DASH WAS PRETTY certain that the worst thing that could happen while moving a dead body was having his nose itch.

He was wearing full personal protection gear including a cap, mask, gown, elbow-length gloves, and booties. There was absolutely no way to reach his nose without risking exposure to the blood on his gloves, and no amount of wiggling against the inside of the mask provided any relief. He even tried rubbing his upper lip against his nostrils, but the itch remained elusive.

Great, and now his nose was *running*.

With a sigh, Dash added one more piece of duct tape to the plastic tarp he'd wrapped the body in and then fled out of the room. He'd left another tarp on the floor just outside the door, and there he stood to strip out of his gear.

He knew he'd have to bag up the soiled items and put on a whole new set to finish the job, but he had to do something about his nose.

Once the soiled gear was safely tucked into a trash bag, he grabbed his handkerchief out of his pocket.

His mentor, Mel, had been right to tell him to always carry a handkerchief for exactly these kinds of situations, though it was Dash's idea to stuff wads of toilet paper into his nostrils to stop any future drips. He adjusted his glasses and then put on a fresh set of personal protection gear, glancing into the room to gauge how much more work he had to do.

It was a relatively easy cleaning job—just one body.

Sometimes there were more.

A lot more.

But such was the life of a cleaner.

Dash was the latest in a line of professionals going back almost a century who specialized in making unwanted problems—*bodies*—go away. Included in the purchase of said service was the very discreet disposal of said problem and eliminating any and all forensic evidence.

The first cleaner was named Melvin Dashiell Purvis, and rumor had it he got his start by making problems go away for the likes of Arnold Rothstein and George "Bugs" Moran. It was an unfortunate coincidence that one of the most famous law enforcement agents of the time just so happened to also be named Melvin Purvis, so the original Melvin opted to start going by M.D. Purvis instead.

This led to even more confusion, however, as M.D. was of course the abbreviation for a medical doctor. Given the nature of the work, many assumed that Melvin was indeed an actual physician and would call him to assist with patients who could not risk going to the hospital for fear of being nabbed by the police.

During one such incident with a fatally wounded person, Melvin famously declared, "Ring me back in fifteen minutes and then I'll take him off your hands!"

From that came the cleaner's motto: *We only clean problems, not people.*

Mel, who was the third Melvin Dashiell Purvis, told Dash that it meant it was not their place to get involved with their clients outside of the job. They only required payment and an address, both of which could easily be provided through encrypted online channels.

Mel often complained about the former stress of receiving jobs through fax machines and was a very big fan of modern technology.

He loved sending Dash corny memes and his texts always had a slew of emojis.

Dash was now the fourth Melvin Dashiell Purvis— that is to say, he was the fourth person to use the name for this very specific line of work.

The original M.D. Purvis, affectionately called Doc by his descendants, insisted on passing the name down to the next cleaner. A name was everything in this business, and untrusting men needed a man they could trust, someone familiar and reliable. So, the Melvin Dashiell Purvis legacy was born.

What started with Doc was passed on to Melvin Junior, Mel, and now Dash. Melvin Junior was Doc's biological son, Mel a trusted business partner, and Dash was a young man in the right place at the right time with a strong back.

He was seventeen when he saw an elderly man fighting to get something in the back of a large van. A desire to help turned into the discovery that what the man was moving had in fact been a body. Dash was not fazed by the grisly reveal and instead asked if the man had a job for him.

That man was Mel, and he was happy to hire Dash to help him over at the crematory he owned.

Dash learned to run the necessary machines for a cremation, like the retort and the processor, the best way to fill and package the urns, and how to navigate the sea of paperwork that came along with each cremation. He'd always had an iron stomach and the oftentimes squeamish parts of the job didn't affect him. There wasn't too much to deal with, as the funeral homes who used the crematory had their own staff perform the removals and then deliver the bodies once the paperwork was complete.

It had often made Dash wonder what Mel had been up to the day they met. If they didn't do their own removals, why was Mel picking up a body all wrapped in plastic? Was it someone he'd known personally?

When Dash had finally gotten the courage to ask Mel about it, Mel had just smiled and told him that it was part of a separate business he ran. Dash had wanted to know more, but Mel promised that he'd explain everything when the time was right.

The right time ended up being a decade and some change later when Mel's health was failing and he needed an heir to pass the name to. He sat Dash down beside his hospital bed and told him the incredible story of M.D. Purvis and the others, and how they had inherited the name.

It was more than just a name, Mel had told him, it was a legacy with over a hundred years of prestige tied to it.

Dash missed Mel terribly.

Not that he was dead or anything, no. Mel recovered, left the hospital, and he'd retired to the sunny beaches of Florida. He was only a phone call away at all times, and Mel had reasoned it didn't make sense to have two men named Melvin Dashiell Purvis in the same town.

Because that's who Dash was now—Melvin Dashiell Purvis. He owned the crematory, two cars, and a very nice condo in a modest part of town. It was more than Dash could have ever hoped for...

Though it was quite lonely.

It might have been strange to be thinking about dating while he was dragging a body out to his van to take back for incineration, but Dash couldn't help it. Finding a significant other had been on his mind lately since a few hookup app dates had fallen through and he realized he hadn't had a boyfriend in four years.

It was difficult to make time for a partner, not to mention the fact that he had to lie to them constantly about what he was doing at weird hours of the night. Working in the funeral business made for convenient lying that no one would question—got a job at two o'clock in the morning? Dash would just say he was on call and had to go deal with a rush cremation.

Excuses, however, didn't relieve the tension created by him being an absent boyfriend.

Dash often worked ten to twelve hour days at the crematory, and it wasn't unusual to be out all night if he had cleaning jobs. He'd clean until the sun came up and then have to turn right around and get ready for that morning's cremation. He missed dates, birthdays, anniversaries, and holidays.

When his last boyfriend broke up with him, Dash was so busy that it took him two weeks to realize he'd been dumped.

After Dash packed the body into the van and shut the doors, he considered that he might need to take some more personal time for himself.

Maybe he needed a vacation.

A spa day.

Fucking *something*.

Dash headed back inside to finish cleaning. Removing the body was only part of the job, and now he had to destroy any and all forensic evidence to protect the client and himself. He had to be thorough, and it was extremely time-consuming. Any possible place that could be hiding a stray fingerprint or even a loose hair had to be scrubbed, vacuumed, and then scrubbed again. If the floor was soiled, it along with the padding had to be cut out and destroyed.

He had a few private contractors who would come replace it in just a few hours no matter what time it was.

This particular cleanup job was unique in that the client had put down a shower curtain before—

Premeditated, Dash's mind supplied.

No. Nope. No to the nope.

That wasn't part of the job.

He didn't ask questions. He didn't need to know anything. He only needed payment and the address so he could clean and go home to his stupid empty condo and do it all again the next stupid day.

Wow, he really did need a vacation.

Dash finished up the last of the cleaning and then drove over to the crematory. No one questioned the lights being on or the smokestack going so late, making it the perfect cover for disposing of unwanted problems. Once the cremation was complete, Dash would sift the ashes into bags of concrete mix to give to the same private contractors who helped him with late-night redecorating.

They never questioned what was in the concrete, just like they never questioned why Dash asked them to refloor entire bedrooms at four o'clock in the morning. The money did all the talking, and it was unsettling how easy it was.

Sometimes it bothered Dash.

All of it did, really.

But this was the job. This was what he had to do, and he would eventually pass it along just as it had been passed to him.

One day.

Until then, he had to work.

Dash stayed at the crematory until the cremation was complete and the ashes were safely stashed in a bag of Kwik-Krete. He groaned in frustration when he saw it was already five in the morning, but he figured he could try to crash out for a few hours before coming right back here to start the day.

Home he went, pausing only to check his mail before he headed inside. He was dead on his feet and ready to pass out, but one of the envelopes in the stack of usual junk mail got his attention. It was dark red and didn't appear to have been stamped, but it was addressed to M.D. Purvis.

Curious, Dash opened it to find a letter.

You are cordially invited to The Anonymous.

We welcome you to enjoy a drink, play a game, find a job or two, and maybe even discover someone to pass the time with. However, there are two simple rules: any form of violence, scrimmage, or heated words will not be tolerated, nor will any discussion of The Anonymous outside of its walls. Disregard either of these rules and you forfeit your life. If you think you can follow these guidelines, you are welcome to join us.

Your code is 1317. When you arrive at the Menagerie Hotel, present it to the concierge and you will be brought down to The Anonymous to mingle with the elite.

Dash read the invitation.

And then he read it again.

He'd never even heard of The Anonymous, though he knew of the Menagerie Hotel. He wondered if this was a joke or some kind of prank. He recalled Mel spending a lot of time over at the hotel because there was a bar inside that he liked, but he had never mentioned anything about a secret elite club being hidden there.

He laughed, set the letter down, and promptly fell asleep on his couch.

DASH WOKE up when the alarm on his phone went off, startling him into action. He bolted up from the sofa and then raced into the bathroom to grab a quick shower. He got out, threw on some clothes, and finished getting ready at neck-breaking speeds to head over to the crematory for the day, forgetting all about the mysterious letter.

That is, until he came home later that evening.

He'd had three cremations to do, which was really pushing it since the machine had yet to cool down from being used earlier that morning. He fought with the controls all day to keep the internal temperature from rising too high and shutting the fire off, not to mention he had to keep rushing back into the office to answer the phone because a frazzled young funeral director was freaking out over not being able to find a specific urn on a preneed file that had been written twenty years ago.

Dash did his best to be helpful, but there wasn't much to be done except call the family and explain this particular urn wasn't made anymore and they would need to pick a replacement.

The funeral director cussed him out.

Wonderful.

It was a very, very long day, and Dash finally left covered in sweat and a fine layer of dust that used to be people.

Dash opted for another shower, a much longer one this time so he could actually enjoy the hot spray beating on his sore back, and then he changed into some sweats and a T-shirt to settle down for the evening. He was already planning on ordering pizza and watching mindless television, but a splash of dark red on the floor by the couch grabbed his attention.

The invitation.

Dash picked up the envelope so he could read the letter again, his heart pounding away.

He almost called Mel right on the spot to see if he knew what this Menagerie and The Anonymous thing was all about, but the letter was very insistent on not discussing it. Dash was paranoid enough to reason that if The Anonymous knew what Dash did and where he lived, they were probably capable of tapping into his phone or bugging his home.

No, that was crazy.

Wasn't it?

Dash wondered how long it would take him to drive over there—now *that* was crazy. He was really thinking about going tonight. That bit about *discovering someone to pass the time with* was weirdly tempting. Trying to date through conventional channels hadn't worked out well for him, but maybe some unconventional ones would prove more successful.

It wasn't that Dash wasn't attractive. He was a tall Black man with warm brown skin, short coiled black hair, and he'd always been told he had beautiful eyes and a great smile. The physical nature of his jobs kept him in fit shape and he'd been blessed with a trim, athletic build. Good looks, however, had never been enough to help him get around the lying constantly about his schedule.

The very idea of dating someone that he wouldn't have to lie to about his late-night work schedule held a lot of unexpected appeal. Dash didn't want to make wild assumptions, but he was pretty sure the other members of The Anonymous would likely work in criminal fields. It would be refreshing to talk to someone about his job in a real and honest way.

Yeah, baby, had a real long day, had to pull someone out of a bathtub. Oh, you'll give me a massage and you're going to order dinner for us? Mm, that sounds great, baby, thank you.

Okay, maybe not, but...

There was a chance.

Dash was already running back into his bedroom to change. One perk of working in the funeral business was that Dash had quite a few very nice suits in case one of the funeral homes he cremated for needed some help with services. One was a gift from Mel when Dash first took over the name, a blue sharkskin suit from Brooks Brothers he only wore for special occasions.

Going out to possibly shack up with a fellow criminal felt pretty special.

He stuffed the invitation in his coat pocket, grabbed his keys, and away he went. Having lived in the city all his life, he knew exactly where the hotel was. He parked, adjusted his suit, checked his bowtie, and wiggled his glasses even though he had just pushed them up his nose moments ago.

It was time to head inside.

The Menagerie was a grand hotel built in the 1800s with ten floors, each punctuated with long rows of framed sliding sash windows and multiple layers of corbels, brackets, and arches all the way to the top. It reminded Dash of a fancy cake, though he couldn't recall any cake ever feeling ominous before.

The lobby was equally intimidating, and Dash nearly tripped over a chair because he was staring up at the incredible vaulted ceiling.

At its center was a massive chandelier flanked by stained glass panels. Elaborate art nouveau moldings spread out like a web from there, framing the countless murals interspaced in between them. It was reminiscent of the Sistine Chapel in both colors and complexity, though Dash didn't linger for too long.

He didn't want to look like a tourist.

He had been invited here.

Well, not *here* specifically, but somewhere special hidden within.

Technically speaking, he was probably not the first Melvin Purvis to be invited here, and he needed to be cool.

He was a professional, for fuck's sake. He could do this.

Dash hurried across the lush red carpet to the front desk, and he offered the concierge a strained smile. "Hello. I'm here for... uh..."

"Of course, sir," the concierge said politely. "Your code, please."

"Code?"

The concierge cleared his throat.

The invitation!

Dash turned to pull the envelope out of his pocket to check the code as discreetly as he possibly could. He felt silly for not having memorized it, and he realized he probably looked like a kid fumbling with their fake ID trying to buy beer.

The concierge was smiling with the practiced patience of a kindergarten teacher who was warning a student not to eat glue for the tenth time, and it didn't make Dash feel any better.

"Thirteen-seventeen," Dash said.

"Very good, sir. Right this way, Mr. Purvis." The concierge came around to lead the charge across the lobby toward a lone golden elevator.

Stealing a final glance up at the extravagant ceiling, Dash followed behind and hoped he was exuding more confidence than he felt. He flinched when the elevator doors closed, and he watched the concierge hit the button for the lower level. It was a fast trip down since it was only one floor, and Dash froze when the elevator dinged to signal their arrival.

"Have a good evening, sir," the concierge said. "Enjoy yourself."

"Uh, thank you." Dash forced a smile. "I will."

The elevator doors opened to reveal a dark and surprisingly modern lounge, and Dash took a deep breath before walking out, heading straight to the bar.

Every inch of the space oozed luxury, from the plush leather chairs and glass-top tables arranged in cozy circles to his left to the chic golden lights illuminating the wares of the bar to his right. Two bars, he saw now as he sat down in the first available seat, lining the wall with a door in between. Everything was decorated in rich browns and blacks, and there were small splashes of gold all throughout that painted a picture of reserved but hip opulence.

Even the bars themselves had golden lights running just beneath their tops for an added flair, and the barstools had thick leather seats.

Dash barely had a second to take it all in before a bartender materialized in front of him.

"Good evening, sir," the bartender said. "What will you be having this evening?"

"Uh." Dash hesitated.

He was usually a beer and nachos sort of fellow, but the unexpected grandeur of the current locale called for something a bit stronger.

"Jack and Coke, please," he replied. "Double."

"Of course, sir. Right away."

"Thank you."

While the bartender was making his drink, Dash turned in his chair to get another look at the room.

Off in the distance, he heard the crack of billiard balls and some jovial chatter, and there were men in suits sitting at a large booth at the back of the room. He tried not to stare, but he was fairly certain he'd seen a few of them on the news before.

"Here you are, sir." The bartender brought him the drink, placing it before him on top of a napkin. "Please let me know if you need anything else."

"Thank you." Dash tried not to gulp it immediately, but his nerves were not cooperating with the plan to act cool and clearly needed some lubrication.

It was going to be fine. He could do this. He was a pro.

He glanced back at the men at the booth, and one of them caught his eyes and sneered.

God, no, this was terrible.

Dash diverted his eyes to his drink, fighting not to grimace.

He looked like a little kid sitting in a high chair. He wasn't going to get laid here. He was probably going to get his ass kicked. This was a mistake. He just needed to go home and—

"New around here, kid?" An older man with a gray beard who had been sitting at the booth was now standing right beside him, offering a smile that was a little too friendly.

"Something like that." Dash cleared his throat and then offered his hand. "I'm Melvin Purvis."

The man's face lit up in surprise and recognition. His smile was sad now, but he said, "It's a pleasure to meet you, Mr. Purvis. I, uh, trust that the number is the same?"

"The same," Dash confirmed.

"I will have some business for you soon," the man said. "My name is Dio Capelli."

A senior lieutenant in the Capelli Family, and a long-time customer—Dash recognized the name immediately.

"Of course, sir," Dash said. "I'll be happy to have you back."

"Good. We're expecting a change in management soon. Nothing too serious of course, just some disagreements in, uh, our finance department. Be expecting my call."

"Looking forward to it, sir."

Dash understood the song and dance behind what Dio was saying at once. He was having trouble with some of his men and they were going to become a problem soon, the very sort of problem that Dash dealt with. Maybe it hadn't been such a bad idea to come out after all.

The sneering man from the booth was walking over to join them, and Dash's stomach tightened.

He was *gorgeous*.

He was tall and broad with long dark hair, sharp features carved from rich olive skin, and bright hazel eyes that rivaled the glitter of the surrounding golden decor.

Dash knew he smelled good. The man just *looked* like he smelled spicy and wonderful, and Dash's fingers clenched the sides of his glass as he tried to resist the wild urge to reach out and pet the man's wavy hair.

"Come here," Dio said, waving the man over. "I want you to meet somebody."

"Sure." The man glanced over Dash as if he was a bug, and he sneered again.

Dash didn't care. Even making that awful face, the man was beautiful. He could easily see himself passing time with that man in a variety of intense positions.

"Mel Purvis, this is my nephew, Tommaso Capelli." Dio smiled. "Tommy, this is Dr. Melvin Purvis."

"Doctor, huh?" Tommy offered his hand for a polite shake.

"Long story." Dash shook Tommy's hand. "You can just call me Dash."

Tommy grimaced at the presence of unexpected moisture, and he wiped his hand off on his pants. "Yeah, looks like you just *dashed* all over my hand."

"Sorry! It was, uh, the condensation from my drink—"

"Don't worry about it." Tommy smirked. "I'm sure you'll be able to clean it up."

Dash quirked a brow. He wasn't sure if that was a joke about his job or not, but he didn't care. He still wanted to get to know this man very well, preferably with no clothes on.

"Get it?" Tommy grinned. "You can clean it up? Seeing as how you're the maid, right?"

"The *maid*?"

On second thought, no, Dash didn't want to fuck him.

He wanted to kill him.

CHAPTER 2

"YEAH." Tommy winked slyly. "I bet you'd look real cute in one of those little uniforms."

Dash's cheeks heated up, and he tried to stay cool.

Tommy had just insulted him mere seconds ago, but now he was flirting with him. It could be a trick of some kind, just another joke being lined up at his expense, but Dash wasn't sure. The slow way Tommy was licking his lips was definitely sending the right signals, but he didn't want to say the wrong thing here.

Especially in front of potential clients.

"Show some fuckin' respect!" Dio clapped the back of Tommy's head. "Mel Purvis has been a name in this town for fuckin' years. He's not one of your little skank boyfriends. Behave yourself."

Tommy didn't seem affected by the smack, saying calmly, "I don't think Mr. Purvis wants me to behave."

"Keep your mouth shut," Dio warned.

One of the other men back at the booth waved, snapping his fingers impatiently.

"I'm comin'!" Dio called to them before turning to give Tommy what must have been the familial sneer. "*You*. I'm gonna be watchin' you. I'll be right fuckin' back." He looked to Dash. "Mr. Purvis, please accept my apologies. My nephew is an idiot."

"That's all right." Dash smiled, finally finding his voice.

"I hope this don't have any effect on any of our future, uh, business arrangements."

"Not at all, sir."

"Thank you. You have a good evening." Dio tipped his head, glared at Tommy, and then turned to hurry back to the booth.

"Wow." Tommy whistled. "You must really be somethin' special to make him kiss your ass like that."

"I have a very unique set of skills that are valued by those in need of them."

"Dead body maid, right?"

"Cleaner," Dash corrected, eyeing Tommy over the rim of his glass. He hoped the alcohol might help pickle his nerves so his heart would stop beating like it was trying to burst out of his chest.

Tommy smiled, and of course, it was perfectly dazzling. "I think maid sounds better."

"A maid can't do what I can."

"Yeah?" Tommy challenged. "And what can you do?"

"I can make you disappear."

"I bet I can make you vanish from this bar."

"And how do you plan on doing that?" Dash shot back.

Dash didn't know if they were fighting or flirting,

maybe a mix of both, but his heart rate was definitely still climbing. He hadn't known quite what to expect when he came here to meet The Anonymous, but wading through a sea of fiery sexual tension with a man he'd just met had not been anywhere on his mind.

Okay, maybe a tiny bit, but—

Tommy leaned in close, so close that his lips brushed over Dash's ear and made him shiver as he said, "By telling you that I'm going to the bathroom in five minutes and I'll be waiting for you in the last stall."

Dash's eyes widened.

Well, that was fast.

"Are you fucking with me?" Dash demanded.

"No, but I'd like to fuck you," Tommy countered. "Or you can fuck me."

Dash scoffed, draining his glass in one big gulp. "You really have no idea who I am, do you?"

"Heard the name before. Know you've been around for a long time." Tommy shrugged, boldly reaching forward to adjust Dash's bowtie. "Always thought Mel Purvis was some old white guy though, not a fine young Black man."

"Careful," Dash warned. "Too many questions will cost your family future business."

"Apologies." Tommy flashed another bright smile, his hand lingering now on Dash's shoulder. "Definitely not trying to offend you."

"What are you trying to do?"

"Take you to the bathroom."

"You are persistent, aren't you?"

"Yes, and very observant." Tommy smirked. "Like

how I observed you checking me out when I walked over here, and how I have observed that you have yet to decline my suggestion for a restroom rendezvous. Which I think means you're interested."

"Maybe."

"Don't be coy now, come on." Tommy squeezed Dash's shoulder. "We can play doctor."

"I'm not actually a doctor—"

"Good. I hate doctors." Tommy winked. "So. Me, you, last stall?"

"You really think I'm down to fuck like that?"

"Like I said, you haven't said no yet."

"No." Dash smiled sweetly.

Tommy laughed and clutched his chest. "You wound me, sir."

"What can I say? I'm a heartbreaker."

"A heartbreaking maid, huh? I think they made a movie about that."

"Not a damn maid." Dash snorted. "You're definitely not getting any company in that bathroom stall now because you're getting on my nerves."

"Hey, hey, I'm sorry. I'm just fucking with you." Tommy held up his hands in surrender. "All in good fun, all right?"

"It's fine." Dash paused. "But you're not getting me in one of those frilly uniforms, much less taking me to the bathroom."

"Hey, I think I still got a pretty good chance of both." Tommy sat down right next to Dash, turning so that his knees bumped Dash's. "You're definitely thinking about it. I can tell."

"Yeah, thinking about what a very potentially bad idea it might be."

"Is anything really fun without being at least a little bad?"

"Maybe." Dash chuckled. "What about just kicking back and watching TV, huh?"

Tommy's brow scrunched. "Are you serious? Like, at home?"

"Yeah. You know, order some pizzas, drink some beer, watch *Ancient Aliens*."

"What?" Tommy suddenly laughed. "That show about aliens building pyramids with Hair Waggle Guy?"

"Hair Waggle..." Dash grinned. "You mean Giorgio Tsoukalos?"

"If he's the dude with the hair." Tommy raised his hand to his forehead, wiggling his fingers to emulate tall, waving locks. "Hair Waggle Guy."

"Yes, he is the guy with the hair." Dash chuckled. "He's a very well respected ufologist."

"With awesome hair."

"He's kinda toned it down the last few years. He said aliens were abducting it."

"So, is that what you're into? Aliens?"

"Aliens, archaeology, history, lots of documentaries." Dash shrugged. "I like movies too. No aliens required."

"Okay, okay. But can we pirate the movie?"

Dash laughed. "Does something have to be illegal for you to have a good time?"

"No, but it's definitely more exciting."

"Yeah? Tell me, Mr. Capelli, is that what you do for

the family, huh?" Dash paused to sip his drink. "Organize mob movie nights? Rip stuff from Limewire?"

"Limewire?" Tommy snorted out a laugh. "Damn. What, are we back in middle school now?" He winked. "I use an Amazon Fire Stick, thank you very much."

"Still pirating."

"Still fun and hey, it's cheap. Because, you know, it's free." Tommy nodded at the bartender, who wordlessly brought him a drink, a martini with extra olives. "For the record, just FYI, I handle the family's books. Used to knock heads around, but then I got a promotion."

"So." Dash grinned. "You're an accountant."

"No, I handle the books. It's different."

"Says the accountant."

"That's real cute comin' from the maid."

Dash chuckled. "You just remember this maid can *literally* make you disappear, okay?"

"If you wear one of those little frilly outfits, I might not mind."

"Oh my God." Dash barked out another laugh.

"How do you do it anyway?"

"Definitely not in a skirt, I can tell you that."

"I've always heard it's like magic. Doin' it in a skirt would be pretty magical."

"Mmm." Dash smiled slyly. "Trade secrets. Can't tell you."

"Some of the old-timers swear it's been the same Melvin Purvis for sixty years and that he's a literal wizard. Magic arts and shit. Sold his soul." Tommy raised his drink. "Can't speak for them, of course, but your smile is pretty bewitching."

"Oh!" Dash laughed at the unexpected compliment and quickly slurped at his drink to buy himself a few seconds to think up a response. He hadn't been flirted with so aggressively in, well, *ever*, and it was stroking a part of his ego that he hadn't realized was itching so badly for it. "You always lay it on this thick?"

"Only when I see something I really want," Tommy said immediately. "They've been letting in a lot of new faces here lately, but you, sir, are exactly my type."

"And what's that? Tall, dark, and mysterious?"

"Maybe." Tommy smiled coyly. "Or maybe I just think you'd look hot with no pants on."

Dash shivered when Tommy's hand fell on his knee. "Let me guess. In a skirt?"

"That too, but how about we start in the bathroom?"

"This with the bathroom again."

"Last stall—"

"You have a one-track mind, don't you?"

"I do right this second." Tommy squeezed. "You seem like you could use some fun, skirt or no skirt. So, why not? Boyfriend?" He grinned. "Girlfriend? Wife, maybe?"

"No, very gay and very single. You?"

"Does it matter?"

"It does to me."

"Well, then you'll be happy to know that I am also single and an equal opportunity troublemaker."

"Bi?"

"Pan." Tommy lifted his drink for a toast.

"All right." Dash lightly clinked his glass against Tommy's.

"We're here, we're queer, and you should really let me take you to the bathroom—"

"Damn!" Dash laughed. "Come on. You know, your chances actually decrease every time you bring it up." He dropped his hand over top of Tommy's. He should be pushing him away, but it was difficult once he felt the warmth of Tommy's skin against his own. The sheer amount of effort Tommy was putting forth to get into Dash's pants was pretty flattering.

"Ah, a romantic, eh? That's okay. I can work with that." Tommy nodded. "So, you like movies, pizza, and beer."

"Look at that. And he listens too."

"I sure do." Tommy finished off his drink, pausing to chew thoughtfully on an olive.

Dash loved watching Tommy's eyes crinkle up as he smiled, and he still couldn't believe that such a hot guy was doing his absolute best to seduce him. No one who looked like Tommy ever gave Dash the time of day, and his ego was officially swollen.

Depending on how things went, it might not be the only thing to swell—

"Hear me out," Tommy declared. "We go to the bathroom—"

Dash laughed.

"No, just listen!" Tommy grinned. "We go to the bathroom, we have ourselves the best time, and then we can go back to your place—"

"Oh, we're going to mine?"

"Mine's a wreck. Trust me. We should go to yours.

Where we can watch a movie and order pizza, drink some beers, whatever you want."

"Why don't we skip the bathroom and just—"

"Because we kinda need to go *right now*." Tommy's grip tightened. "Sort of a limited time offer."

Dash eyed Tommy's hand suspiciously.

"Sorry. You know how it is." Tommy let go, and he forced a smile. "Since I might get swept up at any second, you better grab me while you can. I'm in very high demand."

Dash withdrew from Tommy, warning, "Look, I love what all this is doing for my self esteem, but you are really pushing your luck now."

"I'm sorry." Tommy's brow was dotted with sweat. "I know I can come on a bit strong. I guess I got kind of excited is all. You're hot, you're funny, and you have to be one hell of a somebody to get invited here. I've gotta leave soon, away on business, and I thought maybe we could have a little fun before I had to go."

"Well, when are you going?" Dash smiled. "Are you moving to another country or something? You're talking like you're never coming back."

"I can't tell you except that I'm leaving tonight and I don't know when I'm gonna come back, if ever." Tommy glanced subtly at the rear booth where he'd been sitting.

Dio was watching them from there, and Dash offered him a quick but brief smile, hoping to reassure him Tommy wasn't bothering him.

"Dio mentioned having some trouble," Dash said. "He said he might need to call me soon."

Tommy loosened his tie. "Yeah, and what did you say?"

"Looking forward to it." Dash grimaced. "Wow. I never realized how bad that is to say out loud. That sounds creepy as hell, doesn't it?"

"Just a little."

"Ugh."

"You're just talking about cleaning up murdered bodies. I'm sure that's very normal to be excited about." Tommy grinned. "Probably how everyone would answer."

"Maybe that's why your uncle is staring at us so hard right now. He thinks I'm nuts."

"No, he loves the shit out of you," Tommy said. "You are golden. You don't have to worry about that. He's trying to keep an eye on me. Make sure I don't try to run off."

"Like run off into the bathroom?"

"Exactly! Now you're getting it."

"I don't think I am." Dash laughed. "What are we even talking about now?"

"Last chance for me and you to run away." Tommy reached out to take Dash's hand again.

"Now or never, huh?"

"That's pretty much the idea."

"Kinda romantic," Dash mused. "One last steamy evening over a toilet, never to see each other again?"

"Or you could take me home with you after."

"But not now?"

"You got it."

"You said you have to leave tonight."

"Not if I go home with you."

"But only after we go to the bathroom."

"You, sir, are a genius."

Dash shifted his glasses up his nose, trying to make sense of the predicament. He hadn't had enough to drink for this to be so confusing, but he didn't understand why Tommy wouldn't just leave with him now. He had no idea what was so damn important about going to the bathroom.

Tommy was looking at him so earnestly, as if there was really nothing else in the world he wanted more than to be with him, but how pushy he'd gotten a few moments ago weighed heavily on Dash's mind. That kind of behavior was an instant red flag.

Not to mention how hard Dio and the other men at the booth were eyeballing them right now.

"I will think about it," Dash said at last. He patted Tommy's hand. "Long and hard."

"Trust that yes, it's very long and hard, and it will be waiting for you—"

"Last stall. Got it." Dash smiled through the rising aggravation.

"Oh, you're gonna get it all right." Tommy stood and adjusted his jacket with a sly wink. He leaned in and put his hand on Dash's shoulder, close enough that Dash thought he was going to try and kiss him. "You'll get it however you want it, whatever way you want it, for as long as you want it. I can be very, very good for you."

Dash gulped.

Well, there it was—officially the hottest thing anyone had ever said to Dash's face in the history of ever.

Tommy's eyes lingered on Dash's lips. "You know where to find me."

"Y-yeah. I do."

Tommy leaned in again as if he was going to say more, but Dio was calling for him. He turned to shout back, "One sec!" He smiled at Dash. "Well, I hope I see you soon." He ran his tongue over his top lip.

Christ, it was pierced.

Dash stared at the shiny barbell and forgot how to speak. One of the first boys he'd ever kissed in high school had a tongue ring just like that. His heart tripped over itself, and he had to remind himself to breathe.

Tommy immediately picked up on Dash's fascination, and he clicked the ball against his teeth. He glanced down very purposefully at Dash's crotch in an unspoken promise of where exactly he was willing to put that sinful tongue of his.

It was not fair for one man to be that sexy.

Without another word, Tommy left the bar, doubtlessly en route to the bathroom. He strutted across the floor as if he had every confidence in the world that Dash would be joining him. Dio was trying to get Tommy's attention, but Tommy waved him off, pointing over to the bathrooms as if to say he had to go there first.

Dash noticed Dio and the other men at the booth glancing his way, as if waiting to see if he was going to follow Tommy or not. He absolutely could not do this here, he realized. The last thing he needed was his clients knowing he was so desperate to get laid that he'd jump on some guy's dick he'd just met.

The bartender had appeared again, asking politely, "Would you like another drink, sir?"

"Yes, please."

"Another double?"

"Oh, definitely."

Dash stayed glued to the bar as he nursed his drink, his pulse still fluttering away. He had no idea what the hell had just happened with Tommy, but the man had certainly made an impression on him.

He hated to admit it, but this was really fun. He liked being able to talk to people without hiding who and what he was, and he enjoyed the respect that his name carried. A few other patrons came over to greet him in Tommy's absence, many of them past clients, and they always addressed him with extra reverence as soon as they heard his name.

It was nice.

Much better than picking scrap out of ashes and sweating his ass off in front of the retort.

Sure, a lot of the praise Dash received was actually for his predecessors like Mel, but he allowed himself to enjoy it. He'd never gotten to experience much in the way of appreciation for what he did, either as a cleaner or a normal guy working at the crematory, and he tried not to let it go to his head.

The free drinks were pretty sweet, though.

The promise of sex had been even better, though Dash remained at the bar instead of seeking it out. He wasn't opposed to one-night stands or anonymous quickies, especially since they represented the bulk of his love life these last few years. It hadn't felt right to pursue it here though. After all, the last thing he wanted to do was add "promiscuous" to the Melvin Purvis legacy.

That was part of the trouble, he realized.

He wasn't actually here as himself. He was Melvin Dashiell Purvis, a professional cleaner whose sole function was to take care of unwanted problems discreetly. The real him would have gladly gone to that bathroom with Tommy, but Dash couldn't.

The legacy didn't feel that great now. Instead of being a blessed path lined with praise, it was a miserable stone around his neck he'd have to carry until he was ready to pass it on to some other poor bastard.

Dash decided then it was time to go home.

He hadn't seen Tommy again, and he wondered if Tommy was still waiting for him in the bathroom.

No, that was ridiculous.

It had already been at least an hour since then, but now the desire to check was nagging at him.

Plus he really needed to piss.

Dash found his way to the bathroom, but it was woefully empty, with no sign of Tommy to be found. He used the urinal, washed his hands, and left. Disappointment clung to him as he headed back to the bar.

"Do you know if Mr. Capelli is still here?" Dash asked.

"I believe so, sir," the bartender replied.

"Do you have a pen?"

The bartender slid a pen over. "Of course, sir."

Dash wrote his number—his *personal* number—down on a napkin. He could see this being an awful idea, but the mere thought of Tommy's dazzling smile and his gorgeous eyes dissuaded any lingering reservations.

He handed the napkin to the bartender along with a twenty dollar bill from his wallet. "Could you please see that Mr. Capelli gets this?"

"It would be my pleasure." The bartender smirked. "You have a good night, sir."

"Thanks. You too."

And with that, Dash left.

WHEN DASH'S work phone dinged with an address at one o'clock in the morning, he had been hoping it was Tommy texting him on his personal phone. He'd never met anyone like Tommy, and his brazen attitude was at once grating and intriguing. Dash hadn't been able to stop thinking about him, and it had been Tommy's face at the forefront of his fantasy when he took himself in hand before going to bed.

This was pathetic.

Dash had been too worried about what those other men in the club might think of him, and how it might damage the Purvis reputation, to seize what had been a delicious opportunity right in front of him. Yes, Tommy's behavior had been a bit odd, but he was really hot.

Dash would stress about it later.

He had to go to work.

There were four problems waiting for him at an address about twenty minutes away. He knew the area, and it was a quiet little neighborhood with older homes and thickly wooded yards. Hopefully there would be a garage.

One body was difficult enough to move in secret, but four were going to be a workout.

He texted back the price, waited for confirmation that the payment had been received, and then he dragged himself out of bed to get ready. He knew he was going to get sweaty, so he opted for jeans and a T-shirt, something simple he could move around in easily.

This was not going to be fun.

Why didn't Doc Purvis ever get an assistant to help him move bodies? Why wasn't that part of the stupid legacy?

Dash grabbed an energy drink from his fridge and headed over in his van. He drove along the dark street until he found the right house, and he almost cheered when he saw there was a two-car garage. The house would be unlocked so he could get in, and the first thing he did was quickly park the van in the empty garage.

He didn't know where the cars were for the people who'd lived here. The only thing that mattered to Dash was that they weren't in his way so he could get to work. He'd already put on gloves and booties to cover his shoes, always hyperaware of his presence so he didn't leave any evidence of it behind. He unrolled plastic across the floor to walk on as he searched the house to find the problems.

There was one in the living room and three more in the bedroom. Two of the bedroom problems were clustered right on top of each other, two very tall and very large ones, and Dash lamented the solitary life of a cleaner.

His back did too.

The problem in the living room was the closest, so he started there.

Plastic tarp, duct tape, off into the van.

The single problem in the bedroom came after that, and Dash was pleased that he was making good time. He might even get home before the sun came up today. He was definitely going to have to call a private contractor in for this job because the carpet was ruined, and he was not looking forward to cremating it.

The padding in particular did not smell great while it was burning.

He brought in more plastic to take care of the double problem, the stout men lying together on the floor by the bed. Dash laid out the plastic beside the larger of the two to get it over with, but he paused, looking at the men again. They weren't as big as Dash first thought, which was a relief, but why did they look so large?

Oh!

They were on top of something that was pushing them up off the floor.

Great.

Another body.

Beneath body number three and body number four was a fifth one.

"Definitely gonna be charging you extra, Mr. Capelli," Dash mumbled under his breath. He stepped to the side of body number three, kneeling down to pull the corpse over onto the plastic tarp he'd laid out. He'd have to go back out to the van to get another one for the surprise body.

Who looked...

Familiar.

Dash stopped what he was doing to look at the fifth body, and he gasped.

"No... no, no no." Dash quickly wiped the blood off the man's face, his stomach turning when the body's identity became crystal clear.

It was *Tommy*.

Tommaso Capelli was body number five.

Beautiful, irresistible Tommy, who Dash really wished he'd actually gone to the bathroom with now. On second thought, maybe it was better that he hadn't if Tommy was only gonna end up dead—

"Help..." Tommy whispered.

"Holy fuck!" Dash shouted, scrambling back in terror.

"Help... me..." Tommy whispered again, his eyes fluttering open as he whimpered in pain. "Please... ugh... help..."

Well.

Fuck.

CHAPTER 3

AS A PROFESSIONAL CLEANER, Dash had learned many procedures for dealing with the most unique problems: basement problems, problems up in an attic, problems in tubs and on toilets, problems with spiral staircases, and more. This was the first time, however, that he'd ever had a problem who was still alive.

Dash was driving to the crematory with five bodies, but one was very much not a normal problem as he still had a pulse.

He thought about Doc's infamous quote of waiting to come back when the patient was dead so he could take care of the problem, but Dash couldn't do that to Tommy. Dash *knew* Tommy, at least well enough to have sincerely considered going to the bathroom with him, and the only thing he could think to do was to try and help.

Even if it meant doing something incredibly stupid, like not immediately driving to the crematory.

He instead went home first to drop Tommy off. He

reasoned that Tommy might need first aid, and he had no idea how badly he was injured.

Getting Tommy inside wasn't so difficult as Dash had years of experience moving bodies around, but then Dash didn't know what to do with him. He had a van packed with bodies and bloody carpet and bags of physical evidence right outside he needed to have taken care of twenty minutes ago, and he couldn't risk Tommy getting away and spoiling that Dash had fucked up the job.

Technically, it was Tommy's fault because he'd decided to not be dead and suddenly make a simple job into something much more complicated.

In Dash's panic, handcuffing Tommy to his bed seemed like a great idea. Tommy would be comfortable, safe, and Dash could get a look at his injuries. A very quick and mostly modest examination revealed Tommy had been shot twice, but one bullet had merely grazed his left ear and the other had nipped his side. Most of the blood on him was probably from the other two victims.

Problems. Not victims.

Shit, shit, shit.

Tommy was weak, in and out of consciousness, and he hadn't spoken another word since they'd left the house. Dash didn't think Tommy had lost enough blood to be in shock, but he had to go take care of business before seeing about getting a doctor. He put an energy drink and a few towels by the bedside in case Tommy woke up before he got back.

Dash had to change into a new set of clothes because what he'd been wearing was soaked in blood from carrying Tommy around. He probably should've kept his PPE on, but he reasoned he would have looked more suspicious wearing a big blue gown dragging an obviously wounded man into his home. He had been in such a hurry that he realized he hadn't even bothered to check to see if anyone was out for a late-night jog or walking their dog.

Someone definitely could have seen him.

Shit, shit, *shit.*

At least having been in casual clothes, Dash could try to play it off as if he was taking care of a drunk friend.

A drunk friend who spilled a lot of wine.

Very red wine.

Right.

Dash checked on Tommy one more time, and then he hauled ass to the crematory so he could handle the problems in his van. He didn't even bother cleaning the retort in between burns. As soon as one was done, he loaded in another body and the soiled evidence. He was going too fast, and the fire kept shutting off because it was overheating. He had to slow down and baby it a bit to keep it going, and in the middle of the third burn he realized he hadn't called the private contractor to go fix all the carpet he'd just cremated.

Dash took a deep breath.

This was sloppy.

He was better than this.

Just because there was a very hot man who was supposed to be dead handcuffed to his bed didn't mean he had to act so unprofessional.

He got a hold of the contractor to make the arrangements to replace the flooring, and then he loaded in the fourth body and the last bag of evidence to burn. All of the men had been shot in the head and chest, and he grimaced as he recalled Dio Capelli's comment earlier that evening about cleaning up the financial department.

Wait—didn't Tommy say he helped with the family's books?

Dash had called him an accountant...

Did Tommy know what Dio had been planning?

The text had said four problems, not five. So, was Tommy one of the intended four or an unplanned fifth?

Dash tried to weigh his options.

He could call Mel and ask for advice, but Dash knew he'd already done so many things wrong—like bringing Tommy home, first of all. He knew he should have just left the scene on the spot and texted the client that the problems weren't ready to be taken, but that could have meant sentencing Tommy to certain death. He'd also driven the van to his personal residence and left his bloody clothing back there too.

Shit, shit, *shiiit*.

Definitely not calling Mel.

Dash could handle this.

He was going to finish the cremations, dispose of the ashes, and then go home. He'd bag up the dirty clothing to burn later and figure out what to do about the bloody unconscious man cuffed to his bed.

The sun was coming up by the time Dash finally left. He was exhausted, he needed a shower, and he was absolutely starving. Back in his personal vehicle now, he stopped by a fast food restaurant to grab some sausage biscuits and hash browns, and he got extra in case Tommy was hungry. A side trip was risky, but he knew there wasn't crap to eat at his place.

As Dash stepped through his front door, he paused and listened.

He didn't hear any banging or screaming, so he hoped that meant Tommy was still passed out. Which was also bad, because that meant that Tommy might be really hurt or worse. Dash really didn't want to have to call anyone, but he would if it meant saving Tommy's life. After all, he'd already come this far.

Dash tiptoed into the bedroom, and he was relieved to find Tommy exactly as he'd left him, his chest rising and falling slowly in a peaceful doze. He scowled when he saw how Tommy and his bloody clothes had stained the bed sheets, and he lamented not having laid down plastic or at least a few towels.

It could be worse, he told himself. A lot worse.

Dash set the bag of food down on the nightstand, and then he headed into the bathroom. He grabbed the first aid kit from under the sink, a washcloth that he ran under the faucet to get wet, and more towels. He didn't know why, but he just felt like he needed a lot of towels.

Maybe it was all the blood.

He crept back over to the bed with the supplies, and he sat on the edge of the mattress beside Tommy.

Tommy still appeared to be resting without any distress, and he continued to be gorgeous even covered in blood.

"Tommy?" Dash raised the washcloth to Tommy's brow. He gently wiped at the blood. "Hey, Tommy?"

Tommy's eyelids twitched, but he didn't open them.

Dash continued to wash Tommy's face, taking his time as he scrubbed a bit where the blood had dried. Tommy was really going to need a shower, but Dash could at least get the mess off his face. He cleaned up his ear where the bullet had cut through, and he paused to grab the first aid kit. He didn't know if he had a bandage that would fit an ear, but he thought a fingertip style one might work.

When he turned back around, Tommy was sitting up, his eyes were open, and the cuffs were off.

"What the—" Dash gasped, barely having a moment to reconcile what he was seeing before Tommy tackled him to the floor.

"Who the fuck are you?" Tommy snarled. "Who sent you? Huh? My uncle?"

"Tommy!" Dash shouted, his voice weak from wheezing, as Tommy's weight on top of him had knocked the air out of his lungs. "Dash! It's Dash!"

Tommy stared for a moment, and then he seemed to recognize him. "The maid."

Dash groaned and laid his head back on the floor. "Yes. The fuckin' maid."

The way they'd landed had Tommy straddling Dash's thigh, and Dash's hands were braced on Tommy's broad and very firm chest. Tommy had one hand clenching Dash's shirt collar, and the other was raised as if to strike. Dash was thankful when he dropped it, but they remained frozen as they were.

Not that Dash really minded having Tommy on top of—

"What the fuck happened?" Tommy demanded.

"I was gonna ask you the same damn thing," Dash replied curtly. "How did you get out of the cuffs?"

"I'm a magician. What the fuck was I doing in them?"

"I had a job. I came to clean. I was told there were four bodies—"

"Four?"

"Yeah. You made five."

"Shit." Tommy cringed. "The guys who were with me? They're all dead?"

"And gone."

"One of them was a cop."

"What?" Dash lurched upward. "What do you mean, one of them was a cop?"

"C-O-P," Tommy spat. "You know, cops! Two of them were my guys, my bodyguards. The other guy was a cop."

"Seriously?"

"Yeah." Tommy withdrew and flopped back on the bed with a heavy sigh. "Fuck."

Dash made a face when he saw Tommy had smeared some blood on what was a clean shirt, and there was no telling if it was his or a cop's or whoever else's. It was also on the small rug in front of his bed now, and he sighed. "How about you grab a shower? I got some clean clothes you can borrow—"

"How much do you know?"

"About what?"

"The pile of shit you just stepped in."

"No clue, but I know you're soaking my bed, my rug, and me in DNA evidence I'd rather not have in my fuckin' house." Dash bristled and pointed. "Bathroom. Now."

"Hey! You're finally going with me to the bathroom."

"Very funny." Dash scoffed. "Go on. I'll be right there. Take everything off and put it in the trash can."

"Sir, yes, sir." Tommy gave a little salute and headed that way. "I love taking off my clothes in the homes of men who have handcuffed me while I'm passed out."

"Happens a lot?"

"Every Tuesday!"

Dash snorted, waiting for the bathroom door to shut before he grabbed a trash bag from the kitchen. He stripped the bed and shoved the linens in the trash bag with the rug and the washcloth. When he was sure he'd gotten everything that might be soiled, he joined Tommy in the bathroom. He knew there was a chance he was going to see some skin when he opened the door, but he was not prepared for Tommy standing in the shower stall, leaning against the wall in a provocative pose.

The ring in his cock was a big surprise too.

Dash averted his eyes and reached for the trash can full of Tommy's bloody clothes. He put the entire thing into the trash bag. "Go ahead and get the water going," he said. "Hot. Wash your wounds. We'll dress them when you get out."

"So, how much do you know?" Tommy asked as he fiddled with the faucet.

"About what happened? That there was supposed to be four bodies at that address."

"That's it?"

"Yes." Dash turned his back to Tommy for some illusion of privacy and pulled his shirt over his head. He heard the shower starting. "I found you there, still alive, and well…"

"Decided to bring me home and handcuff me to your bed?"

"Look." Dash grunted. "I didn't know what was going on, and I was in kind of a hurry, okay? Never been anywhere where someone who was dead was also alive."

"Should have just let me take you to the bathroom." Tommy clicked his tongue, whistling low when Dash dropped his pants. "*Damn.*"

Dash ignored him, though the compliment got his face hot. He shoved his clothes into the trash bag with the rest, and he did his best to speak to Tommy and keep his gaze at eye level. "Tell me what's going on. Right now."

Tommy let his eyes wander all up and down Dash's naked body, and he said, "Right now? Blood is leaving my brain and going to my dick—"

"Tommy!"

"Fine." Tommy met Dash's eye. "That night at the Menagerie, I was wearing a wire, okay?"

"A wire?" Dash scoffed. "You're a *snitch*?"

"Listen, *maid*, it gets better. My uncle was real suspicious, and he wouldn't let me out of his sight. After you refused the invitation to my bathroom party, my uncle wanted us to leave and have ourselves a private meeting. The kind of meeting where someone leaves in a body bag. I ran straight to my handler with my guys, but Dio and his men must have followed me. I was pretty drunk, but I remember getting hit, I went down, and well…" Tommy shrugged. "You know the rest."

"Your uncle was willing to kill a cop to take you down?"

"With the song I was singing, he sure was. I told him I knew he was a fuckin' thief and I got proof." Tommy leaned his head back into the spray. "I need to get to my father pronto."

"Your father?"

"Yeah. Leonardo Capelli." Tommy picked up a bottle of bodywash, sniffed it, and then put it back. He grabbed shampoo, sniffed that, and poured some into his hands to lather up with. "I need to get to him as soon as possible."

"Okay, well, good luck with that." Dash cringed, and he turned around so he'd stop being tempted by the delicious vision of Tommy's soapy body. "And close the curtain, you're getting the floor wet."

Tommy rolled his eyes, but he yanked the curtain shut. "How many bodies did you say you found?"

"Including you, five. There were the two guys with you, literally right on top of you, and then one guy off by himself. All in the back bedroom. Oh, and the first one I found was out in the living room."

"Darcey was gonna call for backup. Maybe it was one of his guys."

"Who's Darcey?"

"Was the cop." Tommy groaned loudly. "Your water pressure is amazing. Are you gonna get in here with me or what?"

"No."

"You are no fun, Mr. Purvis." Tommy chuckled. "Fine. Thank you, by the way. For helping me. Not everybody would have done that, you know. Especially in our line of work."

"I only clean problems, not people." Dash smiled. "Besides, I would have had to call your uncle for more money and that would have been—"

"Handcuffs were still kinda weird though." Tommy made a meowing sound. "If you want to get kinky with me, you just have to ask."

"It wasn't like that!" Dash blushed. "I didn't know what was going on and I didn't know what else to fuckin' do! I had to leave you alone in my damn home to finish working, and I had no idea if I could trust you."

"I'll explain everything after you give me a ride to my dad's," Tommy promised.

"A ride?"

"Yeah. In a car. Vroom vroom."

Dash hesitated. "Can't you just call someone?"

"Right now, I don't know who to trust or who might be listening." Tommy poked his head around the shower curtain. "Please. Just give me a ride. I'll pay you whatever you would have been paid to move my body."

"Twenty-five grand."

"Holy fuck, I'm in the wrong business." Tommy grinned. "So, uh, do you want me to wash your hair or scrub your back—"

"If you're done, get out. Check your ears and under your nails first though."

"You know, I almost died last night. I'm feeling very vulnerable. You should hold me."

"Pass." Dash frowned as something clicked into place. "Last night at the bar..."

"You mean when you refused my restroom rendezvous? We can totally make up for that now."

"You just told me your uncle wouldn't let you out of his sight. You knew they were onto you—"

"Yes, I am very clever."

Dash narrowed his eyes. "You were only trying to get me into the bathroom so you could take your wire off, weren't you?"

Tommy paused. "I wouldn't say that was the *only* reason."

Dash's stomach clenched, and he spat, "But that's it, isn't it? Why you got so pushy?"

"Yes." Tommy pulled the shower curtain back and then stepped out onto the mat.

Water streamed from his hair over his Adonis-esque physique, highlighting every thick muscle, and one trickle went straight down to the head of his cock, glistening on the silver ring there.

"My uncle was watching me like a hawk," Tommy continued, "and I got worried he was onto me. When we first got to the club, I tried to go to the bathroom to take it off and he sent a guy to go with me. I faked him out and went to go play some pool instead. But that's when I knew."

"Smooth. Very smooth." Dash took off his glasses and then shoved a towel at Tommy as he pushed by to take his spot in the shower.

"Hey! Don't be mad." Tommy frowned. "I needed to get away from those assholes—"

"And so... what?" Dash aggressively lathered up and

scrubbed his body. "They wouldn't follow you if you were going to have gay sex?"

"I was thinking no." Tommy peeked around the curtain. "When I saw you, the chance to get laid and save myself from getting unalived all wrapped up in one gorgeous mug seemed like a pretty sweet deal."

"Asshole." Dash pulled the shower curtain over to block Tommy's view. "You were just using me. Why didn't you just tell me you needed help?"

"Because my uncle has hearing like fuckin' Superman and he would have heard me."

"From across the bar?"

"That man once heard me fart from the other side of my house and asked if I shit myself, okay? I couldn't risk it."

Dash turned the water off and then reached out to grab a towel from the rack.

"Hey, don't feel bad." Tommy smiled. "You still got to save me, and we can have some fun before you drive me over to my dad's. Got one of those sexy uniforms laying around here somewhere?"

"Let's get going." Dash breezed by Tommy with his towel around his waist, pausing only to grab his glasses from the sink. He kept his eyes forward and off the enticing naked body he left behind, zooming straight into his bedroom to the dresser. He heard Tommy's footsteps approaching, and he said briskly, "I got us some breakfast. Sorry it's probably cold now."

"I can't eat that greasy shit since I got my gallbladder taken out a few months ago," Tommy replied. "Wanna see my scars?"

"No." Dash grabbed a pair of briefs and stepped into them, pulling them up beneath the towel. He yanked the towel off so he could dab off some water he'd missed in his haste, and then he grabbed lotion. He refused to look back at Tommy, even though he knew he was right behind him. "Get dressed. Take whatever you can find that'll fit, and—"

"Hey." Tommy reached for Dash's shoulder, prompting Dash to finally face him.

"What?"

Tommy was still naked, but his expression was surprisingly serious. "I really did like you, Dash. I wanted to get pizza and drink beer and watch some Hair Waggle Guy with you. It wasn't like I was throwing myself on every guy that walked in the door, okay?" He reached out to touch Dash's cheek. "Just you."

Dash didn't feel better. It was much easier to believe Tommy had only been flirting with him to save his own ass than Tommy actually finding him attractive.

Even if Tommy's touch felt amazing and his smile was making Dash's heart flutter in the sweetest way...

He noticed Tommy's wound was dripping blood.

Dash sighed. "Please don't bleed on my floor."

"Right." Tommy withdrew his hand. "On it."

Dash gave Tommy the first aid kit to patch himself up and then finished getting dressed. When he noticed Tommy was having trouble with his ear, he handed him the fingertip bandage. Tommy pouted at him expectantly like a puppy, and Dash begrudgingly helped him put it on.

Tommy spent almost half an hour digging through

Dash's closet trying to find something to wear. Most of Dash's wardrobe was too small for him, and what few pieces would actually fit him were deemed unwearable based on some scale of fashion Dash didn't understand.

He finally settled on a pair of slacks Dash didn't even remember buying and a black T-shirt that was sinfully tight.

Dash opted for a suit, a gray one with a tie this time, since he was potentially meeting Tommy's father, who was also a very high-ranking member of the Capelli family. He decided to think of this as an unusual cleaning job, and he knew appearances were important.

Wait.

Would he be a good cleaner for bringing Tommy back alive to Leonardo or a bad one for failing to let Dio know one of the problems wasn't a problem?

Shit.

Dash reasoned if he got Tommy over to Leonardo's, then he'd be someone else's problem. Period.

He pretended not to notice how Tommy was checking him out while he got dressed or how intently he watched him eat his biscuit as he led the way to his car. He wanted this weird disruption to his regularly scheduled madness to end as quickly as possible, and he still had three not-problem cremations he hadn't been able to attend to.

Tommy's father lived in a private villa almost twenty minutes outside of the city. It was isolated by a few acres and a tall fence. Tommy gave Dash the code to get inside the gate, and Dash was surprised there weren't armed guards with attack dogs. He parked out front of the beautiful home, certain this was going to be another one of those fancy places where he wouldn't want to touch anything.

"What are you doing tonight?" Tommy asked.

Other than giving directions, Tommy had been quiet on the drive over, and Dash was surprised by the sudden question.

"Uh." Dash shrugged as he got out of the car. "Working. Then probably going to sleep. Had kind of a long night."

"I want a do-over." Tommy led Dash toward the front door. "Me and you."

"Excuse me?"

"You don't think I'm really into you," Tommy declared, "so I am going to prove you wrong. I wanna take you out. Wherever you wanna go. We can get some drinks, get some grub, and you can tell me all about how aliens shaped the ancient world."

Dash scoffed, but he was actually touched by the offer. Maybe Tommy really did like him after all, though there were certainly more pressing issues to address before exploring any future romantic avenues.

"Your uncle just tried to kill you," Dash said. "Should you really be, you know, running around the city?"

"That's not gonna be a problem as soon as I tell my dad what's going on." Tommy didn't bother knocking and immediately tried the door. It was unlocked, so he opened it and then ushered Dash to follow him inside.

It was a luxurious space of white marble, tall columns, heavy drapes, uncomfortable looking antique furniture, and elaborate gilded portraits. There was a massive staircase right across from the front door leading up to a second floor with ornate railings that matched the columns that flanked either side of the room.

Dash definitely did not want to touch anything.

"As soon as he hears what Dio did, he is gonna hit the fuckin'—" Tommy stopped short, grabbing Dash's arm. "Floor! Floor!"

"Don't you mean roof?"

"*Floor!*"

Dash's ears rang as a bullet whizzed right by, and he turned his head just in time to see two men with guns charging right at them from the back of the house. He grunted as Tommy shoved him forward, sending him sprawling across the floor. He almost lost his glasses, and he had to stop to push them back up on his face.

"Move! Move!" Tommy shouted as more bullets flew at them, shielding Dash with his body as he herded him behind one of the thick columns lining the side of the room so they could take cover.

Dash ducked down, slapping his hands over his ears to save what precious hearing he had left. He watched in awe as Tommy expertly dove behind one of the antique chairs, inexplicably popping back up with a gun and returning fire at the other men.

One of the men went down and didn't move, and the other ran to hide himself behind the stairs to shoot back. He was shooting blindly, and bullets zoomed all over the place. Dash tried to make himself as small as possible, and he grunted when one errant shot struck the column he was cowering behind.

It ricocheted and hit the adjacent wall, knocking one of the gilded portraits beside him askew. Dash hadn't paid the pictures much attention, especially since there was a literal shootout happening just a few feet away from him, but he kept an eye on this one because he was certain it was going to fall on his head.

And then he realized...

Holy shit.

"Hey, Tommy." Dash's blood froze. "Tommy!"

"What?" Tommy was reloading. "Little busy here!"

"Remember how there were four other bodies at the house?"

"Sort of a weird time to bring it up!"

"You, your two bodyguards, and the cop, right? That's four!" Dash pointed at the portrait. "That guy was number five!"

"What? Are you fucking serious?"

The man hiding behind the stairs shot at them again, forcing them both to duck for cover. The crooked portrait was hit, its glass shattering and then raining down on Dash. He winced as his face burned, no doubt cut, and he shouted, "Yes! I'm serious!"

"You're fucking sure?" Tommy demanded, looking back at Dash with wild eyes. "Absolutely fucking sure?"

"Yeah! Who is that?"

"That's my fuckin' dad!"

CHAPTER 4

"YOUR WHAT?" Dash uncovered his ears to make sure he'd heard Tommy correctly, and he regretted it as Tommy fired back at the man behind the stairs. He thought Tommy had identified that portrait as his father, Leonardo Capelli, and if that was true...

Well, that was a very not good thing.

Tommy was up from behind the chaise and charging brazenly at the man, firing at him to keep him cowering for cover. Tommy must have run out of ammo or perhaps he simply wanted a more personal touch because as soon as he rounded the stairs, he took the man to the floor and began beating him with the gun.

The man screamed, gurgled, and then the only sounds were the wet smacks of metal hitting flesh.

Dash decided to stay where he was until it was over, but he stood to shake the glass off. He waited for Tommy to finish up, but when it became obvious that Tommy wasn't going to on his own, Dash tiptoed over to intervene. "Tommy?"

Tommy was crouched over the man, his hands were bloody, and the man no longer appeared to have a head so much as he had a red blob where his head used to be.

Dash grimaced and tapped Tommy's shoulder. "Hey, Tommy—"

Tommy whirled around, staring up at Dash with tears in his eyes. He swallowed noisily, asking, "What?"

"I'm sorry," Dash said quietly. "I'm so, so sorry."

Tommy's hands dropped, and he sniffed. "You're really sure it was my dad there?"

"Yes. It was him. But he didn't have the beard."

"Shit. Yeah, that's him. He shaved it a few days ago. He just has a mustache now." Tommy sighed. "*Had*, I mean. Where... where is he now then?"

Dash's grimace deepened. "He's been cremated."

"Cremated? Oh, fuck me." Tommy sighed heavily. "He's Catholic. *Was* Catholic." He took the corpse's gun, more ammo from his pocket, and then climbed to his feet. "Stay behind me."

"Wh-what are you doing?"

"I don't recognize these assholes and there might be more." Tommy started toward the stairs. "Maybe they work for my uncle, but they're sure as hell not my dad's men."

"Should... Should we just leave?" Dash frowned. "I would very much prefer not to get shot at again."

"I need to wash up."

"Right."

Dash followed Tommy up the stairs and to a luxurious bathroom. Tommy set the gun on the counter and then turned on the water. He grabbed a bar of soap from the side of the sink and began scrubbing his hands. His expression was dark, torn somewhere between grief and fury, and Dash longed to embrace him.

"Are you okay?" Dash regretted it as soon as he said it, realizing what a ridiculous question that was to ask. "I'm sorry, that was—"

"Hey, hey, it's fine." Tommy offered a very strained smile. "It will be fine. As soon as I gut that motherfucker like a fuckin' fish."

"Who?"

"My uncle, that fucking son of a bitch!" Tommy snapped. He took a deep breath, letting water pool in his hands so he could wash his face. "It's *him*. It has to be him. He's been stealing from the family for fuckin' years. Okay? Fuckin' *years*. My dad knew we were bleeding cash out somewhere bad, he was sure it was Dio, and that's why he sent me over to help with the books."

"To figure out what was going on with the money?"

"Yeah, but I couldn't get anywhere with Dio." Tommy checked his reflection and then grabbed a towel to dry off his face. "I spent weeks trying to crack him, but I got nothing. I could not find anything that proved Dio was the thief, and we were still losing cash by the thousands. So Dad calls his pal Darcey—"

"Darcey the *cop*?"

"Yes! The fuckin' cop!" Tommy groaned. "They went to elementary school together or some shit. They've always been real tight, all right? Darcey wasn't crooked, not exactly, but he was willing to bend a little for my old man. With his help, we were gonna wrap my uncle up like a fuckin' Christmas present, so it was gonna be a big win for everybody. Darcey would arrest my uncle for being a piece of shit thief, my dad was gonna get to clean house and impress the Don, and I was gonna look gorgeous, much to everyone's personal enjoyment." His shoulders sagged, and he bowed his head. "And now..."

Dash's stomach clenched when he saw Tommy's back tremble with the threat of a sob. The man had survived a murder attempt only to learn minutes ago that his father had been killed. Dash knew he needed to turn around and run back home as fast as he could. He wasn't supposed to get involved, and this was a grievous conflict of interest since he had been paid to dispose of Tommy's body. Everything was pointing to a civil war in the Capelli family, and he was risking being on the losing side of it.

That was bad for business and any future in which he desired to have a pulse. He had the Melvin Dashiell Purvis legacy to think about, a legendary name that had survived over a century, and Dash had to be alive to pass it on to the next cleaner.

But he couldn't stand the thought of leaving Tommy...

Shit, shit, *shit*.

For once, Dash wanted to do what *he* wanted to do— the real him, not this mirage created by decades of clandestine service in the shadows. He wanted to do what he thought was the right thing, and that was helping Tommy, a man who had been betrayed by his family and was now in mortal danger.

And yes, Tommy happened to be very attractive and

funny and charming, but Dash told himself that had nothing to do with his decision.

Nothing at all.

Okay, maybe a tiny bit.

Dash put his hand on Tommy's back, asking, "What do we do now?"

"We, huh?" Tommy smiled sadly. "Does this mean you're with me, maid?"

"Sure am, accountant." Dash tried a confident smile. "I'm already going to be in deep shit when your uncle finds out you're alive and I didn't say anything..." He trailed off for a moment, something about the numbers not clicking right in his head.

"You don't need to worry about a damn thing," Tommy promised. "We're going straight to the Don, Olimpio Capelli. We gotta get to him and tell him what's going on as soon as fucking possible."

"Wait a second. Wait, wait, wait." Dash's brain continued to skip until the thought that had been eluding him fell into place. "I don't think your uncle killed your father."

"Huh?" Tommy scoffed. "What are you talking about?"

"He paid me to clean four, not five. You, your two men, plus the cop."

"His name was Darcey, thank you."

"Whatever! You plus two plus one is four." Dash waited for Tommy to catch up. When he didn't seem to be getting it, Dash added, "Your father makes *five*, but your uncle only called me in for *four* bodies. Which means he might not even know your father is dead. Who would your uncle have sent to kill you?"

Tommy whistled low. "That's a long list, but he probably would have come to do it himself."

"Are you sure?"

"Look, none of this matters if we can get to the Don." Tommy took a deep breath. "I can tell him what happened and Dio will be taken care of once and for all. Even if he didn't kill my dad, he sure as fuck tried to kill me and I'm a little sore about that."

"Okay, how do you get a hold of the Don?"

"Normally I call my uncle, but ha! Fuck that!" Tommy rolled his eyes. "We'll have to call his secretary."

"Secretary?"

"He's the Don's *consigliere*. Butch Edwards, but everybody calls him Hagen."

"Let me guess. He's not Italian?"

"Yup. Just like that Robert Duvall guy. He'll be able to get me in with the Don and keep me safe. You too."

"Me?"

"You said it yourself. You're gonna be in deep shit if my uncle figures out I'm alive." Tommy tucked the gun into the waistband of his pants. "I guess we need to do something about the mess downstairs. Only a matter of time before more assholes show up. I'd rather them waste some time lookin' for their fellow assholes instead of walking in on a bloodbath." He grinned. "If only I knew someone who was really good at making bodies disappear."

Dash smirked. "Got any tarps?"

"How many do you need and what color?"

FOUR AND ANY color was the correct answer, and Dash gave Tommy a crash course in cleaning. Tommy didn't have to worry about evidence of his presence being found here since he visited his father's house often, but Dash grabbed some dishwashing gloves and a bottle of bleach from under the sink in the kitchen to minimize and eliminate his own. He would not put problems in his personal vehicle, so Tommy got the car keys off one of the dead men so they could put them inside their own trunk.

Tommy followed Dash to the crematory and then they got to work, putting both men into the retort. The machine was cold so it would take a few minutes to heat up, and Dash made sure he tossed in the soiled evidence from this morning and what they'd gathered cleaning the house. He knew he needed to trash what he had on right now, Tommy too, but he didn't have anything else here for either of them to wear.

"Don't worry about it," Tommy said when Dash told him. "I'll just walk around naked."

Dash snorted.

"Seriously." Tommy smirked. "We can stop by my place. I need to grab a few things anyway before we call Hagen."

"Like what? Shouldn't you go ahead and call him right now?"

"Yeah, one of the things I need to grab is his number." Tommy grinned sheepishly. "Don't judge me.

It's 2023. Who the fuck remembers phone numbers nowadays?"

"Fair."

Tommy glanced at the retort. "So. This is it. The big secret of Melvin Purvis? You just burn them up?"

"Yeah." Dash fidgeted with the controls. "Not so magical once you know, I guess." He paused. "I'm going to assume you want your father's ashes?"

"You still have them?"

"Uh. More or less." Dash grimaced. "I mix them in with concrete and then pass them off to a contractor I work with. But I still have them here. I-I know which one was him." He cringed. "I mean, mostly him."

"Magical."

"I'm sorry," Dash said sincerely. "Really."

"It's okay." Tommy smiled. "Me and him, we didn't always see eye to eye on shit, fought like damn dogs, but he's still my dad, you know? He's my family. I have to make this shit right." His expression dipped. "I'm still trying to figure out what the fuck he was doing there at Darcey's."

"You didn't tell him what was going on?"

"No. After I left the club, I called Darcey first. He told me to stop using my phone, go dark, and said he was calling for backup. Maybe he called my dad, but I don't know. It's... it's kind of a blur. I was pretty fucking blitzed. But I know for sure my dad wasn't there when I went down."

"Did you see who shot you?"

"No. Too fast." Tommy ran his fingers through his

hair and winced when he reached the back. "I think I cracked my head on something."

"You were pretty out of it."

"Well, I thought I was dead until I woke up handcuffed in some hot guy's bed."

Dash chuckled. "Yeah, handcuffs you ninjaed your way out of. How did you do that anyway?"

"I got my own magic." Tommy wiggled his fingers.

"Accountant magic from crunching numbers?"

"Ha ha." Tommy snorted, nudging Dash's arm. "I can dislocate my thumbs and slip cuffs."

"Oh. I thought you picked the lock."

"Nah, that takes too long. Easier to just pop 'em out. Wanna see?"

"What?" Dash grinned. "You dislocating your thumbs or you back in cuffs?"

"Both?" Tommy playfully bumped their shoulders together. "I really do appreciate you helping me. I'll make sure you get paid, all right? Fair and square and shit."

"I'm not worried about the money." Dash was very aware of how close Tommy was now, and it was impossible to resist the magnetic draw between them. "I'm worried about you."

"Me?" Tommy turned so he was facing Dash, his dazzling smile getting Dash hotter than the flames inside the retort. "Come on now. I'm a big boy. I can handle myself."

"Y-Yeah, you can. But there's no telling how much of your family is involved with your uncle and you're alone."

"Am I?" Tommy reached for Dash's hand. "I see you standing right here. And you're pretty damn tough too."

Dash let Tommy weave their fingers together, and his pulse thudded in his ears. "Thought I was just the maid."

"You're a maid with steel fuckin' nuts who kept his cool under fire and didn't flinch scooping brains off the floor." Tommy leaned in, close enough now that Dash could see little specks of gold in his eyes. "That was kinda hot."

"I-It was?"

"Yup. New kink unlocked. Watching you clean up dead bodies like a total badass."

"Christ, you're insane." Dash laughed.

"Probably. But I do think my chances of getting through this shit are a lot better with you." Tommy kissed Dash's cheek. "And I still want that date, you know. Me, you, pizza, beer. Hair Waggle optional."

Dash shivered, his face igniting instantly from the caress of Tommy's soft lips, and he squeezed his hand. "Let's make sure you're not gonna get whacked first, all right?"

"Got it. Don't get whacked, go on date, have freaky weird sex. I'm all over it. Oh, and give my dad's bag of Kwik-Mix a proper burial."

"It's Kwik-Krete."

"Whatever." Tommy laughed. "Maybe this works out, you know? My grandpa, the Don, he actually wants to be cremated. He doesn't care much for the church and always talked about having his ashes taken back to the old country and spread around some vineyard. Maybe one day him and my dad can make that trip together."

"Yeah?"

"Totally! We can make my dad into an ashtray or somethin' to hold him."

Dash grimaced.

"Seriously." Tommy wrapped his arms around Dash in a crushing embrace. "Thank you."

Dash awkwardly hugged back, delicious tension rising in his core as Tommy's strong body pressed flush against his own. His stomach dipped like he was falling and he melted in Tommy's embrace. "You're welcome. I..."

"What?" Tommy nuzzled Dash's cheek.

Dash was so caught up in the rush of Tommy's hot breath tickling his skin that he honestly forgot what he was going to say. He turned his head, breathing in the tease of Tommy's lips ghosting his own as he said, "We've got at least two hours before the cremation is done, and I cannot leave the machine unattended while there's fire inside. State law."

"So." Tommy grinned. "You're telling me we got some time to kill..."

"We are not fucking in the crematory."

"No?"

"No."

"What about kissing, hmm?" Tommy's hands dipped to cradle the small of Dash's back. "Just one very simple, quick and friendly kiss?"

"You really wanna do that right now?"

"I'm feelin' real happy to be alive and I'm not sure how much longer I can go without kissing you."

"Just can't control yourself, huh?" Dash took a deep

breath, trying to gauge how foolish it might be to do that right here right this very second.

"Nope. Sure can't." Tommy's nose brushed against Dash's, and he smiled. "Wanted to kiss you at the bar. At the house. At the car when you rolled that guy's body into the trunk all by yourself. *Christ*, Dash."

"You are so weird—"

Tommy pressed his lips to Dash's, and Dash's brain decided it didn't need to worry about how terrible of an idea this was. The only concern was keeping the slide of Tommy's mouth going against his own as he dug his fingers into Tommy's hair.

Tommy was a patient kisser, kissing seductively slow as he mapped out the inside of Dash's mouth with his pierced tongue. He rubbed Dash's back, and his hands slipped beneath Dash's jacket to fan across his spine as he held him close. A kiss had never felt like this—like a volcano getting ready to erupt, a firestorm bubbling up beneath the surface whose inevitable conflagration was going to be fierce.

"You're so fucking sexy," Tommy murmured, his voice reaching a low pitch that rumbled like thunder, and Dash's hips jerked forward.

"So are you," Dash whispered as he licked at Tommy's lips. "Fuck, so are you."

Tommy kissed him again, steering him out of the retort chamber toward the office. Dash wasn't sure exactly where Tommy was trying to get them to, probably the nearest horizontal surface, but it was hard to help navigate when he was caught up in sucking Tommy's tongue.

Dash grunted when his back hit a wall and then the corner of a doorway. "Mm, easy."

"Sorry." Tommy grinned, readjusting their path so he was backing Dash into the office and up against a desk. "Better?"

"Better." Dash drew Tommy in for another passionate kiss.

The office was small, the space almost entirely occupied by an old metal desk and a tall pair of filing cabinets. A pallet was crammed in the corner beside the door, stacked with bricks and bags of cement.

Dash had spent hours at that desk toiling away over medical examiner certificates and cremation authorizations, and he'd never imagined that he'd be here making out with a hot young mobster after surviving his very first shootout and just cremating two bodies. It was surreal, and he couldn't believe his love life was now bleeding over into his work life.

Bleeding quite literally, considering how Tommy had bled in his bed earlier today.

He kissed Tommy with everything he had, years of frustration fueling his rising passion. He didn't have to lie with Tommy, he didn't have to hide who he was, and it was strangely erotic to kiss someone he'd cleaned up a body with. He could still smell the bleach, the blood, and he wanted nothing more in that moment than for Tommy to tear all his clothes off.

As Tommy directed Dash toward the desk, they both stumbled over the corner of the pallet.

"Shit!" Tommy's foot caught a bag of cement and tipped it over, and then he froze.

"Hey, hey, it's okay." Dash petted Tommy's cheek. "Fuck it, I'll get it later."

Tommy stared at the powdery mess on the floor. His entire body had gone rigid, and his brow furrowed. "Sorry, I…"

Dash realized the reason for Tommy's discomfort, and he took a deep breath. "That's not anybody. It's just regular concrete, okay?"

"I thought it might be my dad." Tommy breathed in deep, exhaling slowly. "Fuck."

"I know." Dash wanted to keep going, but it was clear the moment had been tainted. He politely kissed Tommy's cheek and started to pull away.

"Hey." Tommy hugged Dash's waist. "Where you goin'?"

"Sorry. Kinda figured you needed… I didn't think you'd want this right now."

"Come here." Tommy cupped the side of Dash's cheek, kissing his lips softly.

"Are you sure?" Dash whispered.

"Very fucking sure." Tommy set course for the desk once more, and he grabbed Dash's hips, kissing him deeply.

Dash grunted as he clamored up on the desk, and Tommy pressed firmly between his legs. Dash shrugged out of his jacket, struggling to keep their lips connected when he went for his pants next. He could feel how hard Tommy was, and his own dick was throbbing.

Tommy grinded forward, colliding their dicks with extraordinary precision, and he squeezed Dash's thighs. His kisses were needy, eager, and he was soon panting.

He unzipped his pants, but it was Dash who grabbed his cock.

Dash didn't know what was going through Tommy's mind at that moment, but he understood the basic need to be desired and to feel good all too well. It was a balm for his own aching loneliness, and he hoped it would be a reprieve for Tommy as well.

He stroked their cocks together, thumbing over their slits and playing with Tommy's cock ring. When Tommy grunted encouragingly, Dash focused his touch there and rubbed around the jewelry as he jerked them off.

"Fuck, that's good." Tommy grabbed a hold of Dash's cock, moving in the same syrupy slow rhythm. "Mm, this good? You like this?"

"Yeah." Dash panted. "Mm, a little harder." He groaned when Tommy immediately tightened his grip. "Like that, just like that."

Tommy kissed him, their pumping fists colliding between them as they each sought to take the other over the edge.

Dash knew it would be quick, but he didn't care. He just wanted to come, and he bucked up into Tommy's hand, seeking more friction. He stroked Tommy faster, focusing his thumb around the ring where it emerged just below the head of Tommy's cock. That seemed to be a sensitive spot, and he loved how wet Tommy was getting, his fingers soon sliding in precome.

They pressed their foreheads together, eyes fixed on their frantic stroking, trading breaths as they rocked together.

Tommy gasped, his grip faltering as he tensed. "Dash, I'm..."

"Come on." Dash picked up the pace, his hand a blur on Tommy's dick. He mouthed at Tommy's cheek, and he urged, "Come on, baby. Come for me."

Tommy's breath came out in short puffs, and he shuddered. "Ah, *fuck*."

Dash watched Tommy come, the first pulse shooting over Dash's fingers and then the rest bubbled out around his cock ring. Dash used it to stroke Tommy through the final waves of his orgasm, and he was dying for a taste.

"God, yeah." Tommy growled hungrily, and he rocked into Dash's hand. He jerked Dash faster now, pressing a breathless kiss to his lips. "I wanna see you come. Get that nut, baby."

Dash stuck his fingers in his mouth, licking off Tommy's come as he thrust into his frantic grip. The pressure was awesome, the friction rising fast, and the taste of Tommy's hot come on his tongue drove him headfirst into a fantastic climax. His pulse throbbed in the head of his dick and in his balls as he climaxed, his hips bucking forward as he groaned low. "Fuck, fuck, fuck, *yes*!"

His skin prickled with wondrous heat, his core ached with every wave of pleasure, and he watched his come shoot across Tommy's shirt and then his fingers. Tommy squeezed Dash's dick, trying to wring out every last drop of come, and Dash had to push at his hand for mercy, whining softly.

"Mm, baby." Tommy kissed him, a firm press of lips that lingered.

Dash kissed back hungrily, his face flushed and smiling. "Fuck, that was good."

"Mmm, yeah?" Tommy smiled, and it lit up that dreary office like a thousand suns. "Just you wait. That's just an appetizer."

"Oh?" Dash laughed.

"You bet your sweet ass. That's just to take the edge off until we get to my place." Tommy stripped off his T-shirt since it was already covered in come and then used it to wipe them both down. He teased over Dash's cock until he squirmed, and he chuckled as he kissed Dash. "Sorry. Can't keep my hands off you."

"Resist temptation." Dash smirked. "I still have to wait for the fire in the machine to turn off before we can go."

"Then we can go to my place?"

"Yes. For clothes. And to get Hagen's phone number."

"And sex."

"No."

"Blowjob?"

"*Later.*"

"Hey, that wasn't a *no.*"

CHAPTER 5

WHILE THEY WERE WAITING for the fire in the retort to go out, Dash had to make a few phone calls. He had those three scheduled cremations today, but he didn't see them happening with everything else going on. Even if he had wanted to get some work done, having Tommy here was very distracting.

Dash barely made it through calling the funeral homes to let them know there was going to be a delay because of the way Tommy decided to lounge shirtless around the office. He had to explain to the funeral directors there was an issue with the machine while Tommy nuzzled at his neck, and he promised them that he'd have the cremations done by the end of the day tomorrow.

However this went down, Dash still had a legitimate business to run.

Dash was able to set a new schedule in spite of the many temptations Tommy presented, and getting cussed out by that frazzled funeral director again wasn't so bad with Tommy's kisses to enjoy.

And God, those kisses were *amazing*.

Dash allowed himself to enjoy a few more after he'd checked the machine and confirmed the fire was out so they could leave. Tommy said he was fascinated with the cremation process and wanted to see it from start to finish sometime, though his enthusiasm dimmed a bit when Dash presented him with the bag of concrete containing his father's ashes. He kissed Dash and thanked him, though Dash still felt the need to apologize.

He thought about offering Tommy an urn, but he didn't think the entire contents of the bag would fit.

Maybe a really big vase.

Tommy carried the bag in his lap as they drove over to his place, a newly constructed luxury apartment building in the heart of downtown that required a code to get through the gate.

"Don't suppose you know what happened to my car?" Tommy asked woefully, eyeing an empty numbered parking space. "I had it over at Darcey's."

"Sorry," Dash replied. "There weren't any cars at the house when I got there."

"Dammit. I really liked my car." Tommy gestured to the space. "Just park here."

"Where's the office? Aren't you going to need a key?"

"Nope." Tommy winked. "I have a space door."

The space door turned out to be a door with a fancy panel that unlocked with a pin number instead of a key.

Tommy opened the door and then ushered Dash

inside, saying, "I'll need to use your phone. No telling where mine is at."

"That's fine." Dash glanced around. "You can use my work phone."

The apartment was modern, chic, and Dash was drawn to the fancy entertainment center in the living room. The massive television was flanked by sleek glass shelving that housed every gaming console Dash could think of and a few he didn't think he'd ever seen before. The sofa and its matching recliner were black leather, and the coffee table had a funky glass top shaped like a kidney bean.

"Make yourself at home." Tommy smiled. "I'll just be a second. Unless..." He winked slyly. "You want me to show you the bedroom?"

Dash chuckled. "I'm sure I'll see it later."

"Fine. Suit yourself." Tommy leaned over to smack Dash's ass.

"Hey!" Dash laughed.

"Be just a sec!" Tommy flashed a cheeky grin and then headed into the kitchen. He came back out with a beer in his hand and no concrete bag, and then he walked through another door, presumably into the bedroom.

Dash finished looking at the gaming consoles and then wandered into the kitchen. It was all marble countertops and stainless steel appliances, and he noticed that Tommy had set the bag of concrete next to the fridge on the counter.

Maybe he could help Tommy turn his dad into one of those garden stepping stones or something.

Tommy emerged wearing a suit with no tie, his expression grim. He perked up when he saw Dash, and he greeted him with a kiss. "You need somethin'? Thirsty?"

"No, I'm all right." Dash touched Tommy's cheek. "You okay?"

"Just got a lot on my mind, babe." Tommy held up a piece of paper. It looked as if he'd been using it as a coaster for quite some time. "Let's finish this shit right now, all right?"

Dash reached into his pocket for his phone. He unlocked it and then offered it to Tommy. "You really think a phone call is gonna fix everything?"

"It's sure as fuck a good place to start." Tommy took the phone, glancing at the paper and dialing quickly. He clicked the speaker button, waiting until the line rang before heading over to the fridge. "Come on. Pick up, pick up, pick the fuck up—"

"Hello?" an older man answered.

"Hagen!" Tommy greeted cheerfully. "Fuck, am I glad to hear your voice."

"Tommaso?" Hagen sounded surprised. "Is that you?"

"Yeah, it's me. Who were you expecting, the Easter Bunny?" Tommy snorted and opened the fridge.

"Dio told us you were dead!"

"Yeah, I'm sure he's been tellin' you guys a whole lot of things." Tommy grabbed two beers and tried to hand one to Dash.

Dash politely shook his head.

Tommy shrugged, carrying both beers with him into

the living room as he continued, "He probably failed to mention that he's the one who tried to fuckin' kill me 'cause I figured out he's been stealin' from the family. Oh, and my personal favorite, that he's the *bastardo* who killed my fuckin' father."

"Leo?" Hagen gasped. "Leonardo is dead?"

"Yes." Tommy cut his eyes at the bag as he sat on the couch. "He's dead, I'm fucked, and I need to talk to the Don as soon as possible." He set one of the beers down so he could open the other. "I want Dio fuckin' six feet under and I need some protection until this bullshit blows over. Somethin' real nasty is going down, and I don't know who else might be involved."

"Okay." Hagen was quiet for a moment. "Where are you now?"

"With a friend."

Dash sat beside Tommy, offering what he hoped was a reassuring smile.

Tommy lifted his beer toward Dash in a silent toast and then took a swig.

"Who is it?" Hagen demanded. "Is it someone you can trust?"

"Yeah. I trust him." Tommy smiled at Dash. "I'm good for now, okay? I promise. But I need to speak to the Don. Put him on the phone."

"The Don is..." Hagen cleared his throat. "He is at an appointment."

"What kind of fucking appointment?"

"A fuckin' private one! For Christ's sake!" Hagen groaned. "Listen to me, kid. Dio is out there telling everyone with a pair of ears that you're a snitch and that you were working with the cops. He said he was going to take care of it—"

"Yeah, by trying to fuckin' *kill* me."

"What happened?"

"Look, I will explain everything to the Don whenever he's free from his *appointment*." Tommy rolled his eyes. "Any idea when that's—"

Dash quickly pushed the mute button.

"Hey, what are you doing?" Tommy frowned.

"Ask him if Dio has said anything about your father," Dash said urgently. "If he's out there bragging about killing you, did he admit to killing him?"

Tommy's eyes widened, and then he nodded.

"Tommy?" Hagen asked worriedly. "Are you still there?"

Tommy pressed the mute button again. "Yeah, I'm here. Hey, quick question."

"What?"

"Dio say anything about my father?"

"What do you mean?"

"Did my piece of shit uncle have the fuckin' balls to admit he killed my father?"

Hagen paused. "No, but I know the Don asked to see Leonardo in person after Dio gave us the news about you. He hasn't been by here in probably a week or two, and Dio said he hadn't been able to get a hold of him on the phone at all today. Then he started ranting about the money that's gone missing. If what you're saying is true, Dio is trying to cover his tracks by getting everyone to focus on you."

"Wow. Sure. And what was my uncle gonna do? Call

my dad and apologize for killing me?" Tommy scoffed. "That's *bullshit*."

"Don't suppose you have proof?" Hagen sighed. "I'm sorry, kid, but it's your word against Dio's right now."

"Fuck yeah, I got plenty of proof!"

Dash mouthed, *You do?*

Tommy shrugged helplessly.

"Tell me what you have so I can tell the Don," Hagen said firmly. "Let me help you."

"You can help me by letting me know when I can come talk to him," Tommy countered before promptly hanging up.

"So, exactly what proof do you have?" Dash quirked his brows.

"Fuckin' jack and shit." Tommy grimaced. "I maybe lied about having all this magical proof, but I would say Dio tryin' to kill me makes him guilty as fuck, don't you think? And my dad was certain that he was the fuckin' thief. But if you want actual physical proof, like an audio recording or a signed confession, uh, not so much."

"Without proof, it's your word against Dio's, and you were technically working with a cop..."

"I had to say somethin'! Hagen doesn't believe me. But I can convince the Don. I just gotta talk to him. He knows my uncle is a greedy prick. He'll believe me."

"Isn't it a tiny bit strange that Dio isn't claiming responsibility for killing your father?"

Tommy sipped his beer. "Maybe he's waiting. He might be trying to thin out the herd, you know? People he knows are loyal to my dad. We didn't exactly see any friendly faces out at my dad's place, you know. And it was like those fuckers were waiting for us. Well, not *us*, but you know, more of my dad's people."

Dash's brow furrowed.

"What?"

"Four is not five."

"Still on that, huh?" Tommy chuckled. He finished off the first beer, now reaching for the second.

"You leave the club to meet up with Darcey. Dio sends his guys after you." Dash scooted closer. "They hit the house, kill Darcey, your men, you—"

"Marco and Hall."

"Who?"

"My guys. That was them."

"Right. So. They kill Darcey, Marco and Hall, and you." Dash shrugged. "Why kill your father? And why kill him if Dio was only ordering in a cleaner for four bodies?"

Tommy frowned, taking a thoughtful drink of beer. "All right. Could be that my dad walked in after the fact. After me and everybody else was down, I mean. Maybe Darcey did call him and he was coming over to help or somethin'. Tell my uncle's men to stand down and shit, that their boss was a fuckin' traitor."

"Okay, so let's say they're loyal and they won't betray your uncle, so they kill your dad. Why not tell Dio?"

"Maybe they were afraid Dio was gonna kill them for killing his brother. Maybe they left my dad there for you to find, thinkin' you'd report it in to Dio to get more money for the fifth body he failed to mention."

"Right. Which I didn't since, well, you were alive."

"Huh." Tommy stretched his arm over the back of the

couch, smoothly sliding it over Dash's shoulders. "How very interesting."

"Also, it's worth noting I don't actually know if it was your uncle who hired me."

"What do you mean?"

"All I get is a text message from an encrypted number with an address and how many to clean. I name the price, they pay, and I only go once payment has been confirmed." Dash shrugged. "I *assumed* it was your uncle because of what he said to me that night at the bar."

"What exactly did he say?"

"That he was gonna have some business for me soon. Something about trouble in the financial department."

"That fucker." Tommy scoffed.

"What I'm saying is we don't actually know it was your uncle who called me."

"Hagen just told us Dio is blabbing to everybody about killing me. Maybe he didn't push all the little buttons to actually send the message to you, but this was him. No doubt."

Dash held up his hands. "Okay."

Tommy pulled Dash in closer and kissed his forehead. "Look, it's very sweet that you're so worried about me, but don't be. I promise I'm gonna be okay and we're gonna have so much sex. We can even have some before we go see the Don—"

"We can, huh?"

"Absolutely." Tommy grinned.

"How long do you think it's going to take Hagen to call you back?"

"I dunno. Maybe a few hours. Definitely long enough for me to bust all up in—"

Dash snorted. "How about we eat first?"

"I could sustain myself for days on a diet of your sweet primal juices."

"That is gross and definitely not true."

"Only one way to find out." Tommy wagged his brows enticingly.

"What about we try some Grubhub instead?" Dash didn't miss how Tommy was staring at his lips.

"Yeah? Wanna dine in and then I'll eat you out?"

Dash's loins clenched. "You always come on this strong?"

"No. But I really like you, and I feel like we've been bonded by the power of being shot at, body removal, cremation, and a mutual interest in UFO guys with fabulous hair."

"Wow. Yeah." Dash's pulse sped up as Tommy leaned in. "Hard to argue with that."

Tommy kissed him, a spectacular seduction of lips and tongue, and he slid his hand over Dash's cheek. It would have been very easy to give in to those hot kisses, but Dash's immediate priority was getting something to eat.

Food first, then dick.

"So." Dash leaned back, more than a bit flushed. "Uh, what do you like to eat?"

Tommy grinned.

"For *food*."

"Italian, obviously. Thai, Greek, Chinese." Tommy shrugged. "I love food. I just gotta be careful these days because of my stupid gallbladder. You know, since I don't have one."

"Whatever is fine by me." Dash smiled when Tommy took his hand. "What about Chinese? Anything there you can eat that's not gonna upset your stomach?"

"For egg rolls, I am willing to risk it."

Dash brought up the food ordering app on his personal phone so they could pick and choose what they wanted to order, and he could almost pretend this was a normal date with a normal boyfriend—not two guys who had spent their day being shot at and burning bodies.

Thinking of Tommy as his boyfriend was a little fast, though their current circumstances had certainly brought them close in a very short amount of time. He hoped they were going to have the opportunity to explore a potential relationship later, but first they had to fix the mess that had brought them together.

And not get shot.

And also not get arrested.

But mostly not getting shot.

Tommy turned on the TV, scrolling through millions of channels before he declared there was nothing to watch. They chatted instead, the conversation light despite the tense situation, and Dash got up with Tommy when he wanted to grab another beer.

He hovered by the counter and very purposely avoided looking at the bag of concrete while Tommy dug through the fridge.

There was a knock at the door.

"I'll get it." Dash headed to the door.

"Wait a second." Tommy was still neck deep in the fridge.

"I'll check. Don't worry." Dash glanced through the peephole, but he only saw a man standing there holding a plastic bag. He reached for the doorknob.

"Hey!" Tommy shouted. "Wait!"

Dash had already opened the door, but he paused, turning to frown at Tommy. "What?"

"Don't—!" Tommy's eyes widened.

Dash looked back to the delivery man, and he froze, finding not a big bag of food being shoved in his face but a gun. He didn't have time to scream or even blink, and there was a sudden *thunk*.

Tommy had thrown a knife from the counter, and it had landed directly in the man's right eye.

Dash did scream then, a quick panicked shout as he scrambled back from the door. He shoved the gun away from his face, cringing as it fired. Another man was barging in now, tall and bearded, and he roughly slammed Dash against the door as he tried to force his way by them both.

Dash's head hit hard enough to daze him, and he squinted against his blurred vision, trying to see what was happening and keep the second man from getting in.

The delivery man was unintentionally helping by blocking the way and not moving, perhaps in shock because of the knife currently sticking out of his eye. His gun fell from his hand when the second man finally shoved him to the side and then rushed by him into the apartment.

Tommy was there to intercept the second man, already grabbing the man's gun that he was attempting to aim. "Dash! Get the other gun, get the fuckin' gun!"

Dash's head was spinning and his vision was so blurry—shit! His glasses! His glasses must have fallen. He couldn't see anything except fuzzy shapes and lines, and he hissed in frustration.

Tommy and man number two had taken their struggle toward the living room, and Dash only spared a quick glance to make sure it looked like Tommy was winning. He couldn't see crap, and he dropped to the floor, feeling around for anything that looked like it might be a gun or a pair of glasses.

The delivery man howled as if he was just feeling the effects of having a kitchen knife where no kitchen knife should be, and he fell to the floor, clawing at his face and kicking his feet.

One of his feet caught the side of Dash's head, and he groaned, raising his arm to shield himself from future blows. He managed to block a few, but he soon changed the direction of his search to avoid the delivery man all together.

He couldn't clearly see what was happening with Tommy and the second man, but he could hear the grunts and angry curses. There was a crash as one of them threw the other into the glass shelving unit holding the gaming consoles, and Dash really hoped it was Tommy who had done the throwing.

Dash crawled forward, and there was something under his elbow that made him pause.

His glasses!

He cackled triumphantly as he put them on, the world finally coming into focus just in time to see Tommy heaving the second man into the glass top coffee table. The table shattered, the man groaned in pain, and Tommy silenced him with two quick shots to the head.

Dash grimaced, wishing he'd waited about ten seconds before putting his glasses on.

Tommy hurried over and then dropped to one knee beside him. His nose was bloodied, his hair was mussed, but he otherwise seemed unhurt. He grabbed Dash's arm, shouting over the delivery man's pained cries, "Are you okay? Are you hurt?"

"No, no, I'm okay."

"*What?*"

Dash grunted as Tommy heaved him up to his feet, and he tried to raise his voice, yelling, "No! No, I'm—!"

Tommy groaned and shot the delivery man, and then the screaming stopped. "Sorry, what? I couldn't hear you."

"I think it's time to leave."

"I think you're right."

Tommy rushed Dash out into the hallway, and Dash nearly tripped over another body.

"Shit!" Dash stared down at an old man in his sixties, and his heart clenched realizing this must have been the actual delivery man. He couldn't tell if he was alive or not, and he knew they didn't have time to check.

Tommy was already on the move, pausing only to turn around and grab the gun from the floor.

"Hey, where the fuck was that damn thing?" Dash asked sourly. "I looked everywhere for it!"

"By the edge of the rug," Tommy replied as he looped arms with Dash. "No clue how you missed it."

"Fuck off."

"You're a much better maid than you are a gun-finder." Tommy whisked Dash to the stairs.

"Are you okay? Are you hurt?"

"No."

"Good. Because when we get out of here, I'm kicking your ass for calling me a maid again."

"Can't wait." Tommy flashed a quick smile.

They raced down the stairs and then flew out to the car. They had mere minutes until the police arrived, maybe only seconds. The gunfire had to have drawn the attention of the whole floor if not most of the adjacent building, and they both knew they had to get out of there fast.

Dash's fingers shook so badly that he had trouble getting the car started, and he took several deep breaths to help navigate the insane flood of adrenaline still pumping through his system.

"We're good. We're alive." Tommy squeezed his shoulder.

"For now." Dash sighed and as calmly as he could, he backed out and then drove toward the gate. He could hear sirens wailing close by, and the gate took an eternity to finally open before he could drive out of the apartment complex. He didn't see any police, but he didn't feel safe yet.

"Shit, shit, shit." Tommy exhaled sharply. "This is fuckin' insane. I can't believe my uncle tried to kill me. *Again*."

"Why would he send someone to kill you if he already did?"

"Obviously he knows I'm not dead. Maybe he finally figured out his guys at my dad's place aren't just playing the world's longest game of hide-and-go-seek." Tommy cringed. "He might know you're helping me."

"Great."

"Look, it's gonna be okay. My family still has connections. That little mess at my apartment—"

"The *little* mess? You mean the two dead bodies with the grossly negligent amount of forensic evidence we both left behind? *That* mess?"

"Have a little faith, babe. I'm gonna make sure it's taken care of."

"Yeah? And how are you gonna do that from hiding under a rock?"

"I was thinkin' I could do it from your place and then do you."

Dash sighed haggardly.

"We need somewhere to lay low until Hagen calls me the fuck back. Which means we either go to your place or we shack up in a hotel."

"Don't you have safe houses? Hideouts?"

"Yeah," Tommy replied with a snort. "And my whole family knows about every last one. I have no idea who to trust right now except me, you, Hagen, and the damn Don. Everybody else is fuckin' sus."

"*Sus?*"

"Yeah, you know, sus." Tommy rubbed Dash's leg. "It's what the kids say these days. You really need to get out more."

"Right." Dash fidgeted. "What about the bodies at your apartment? The police are gonna be looking for you now. Probably me too since I'm sure someone saw us together and I bet that fancy apartment has lots of cameras. Shit, there's no way we'd be able to get in there and out with the cops there—"

"Hey, hey. Don't you worry your pretty little head about it, babe," Tommy soothed. "You might be a wizard at making bodies disappear, but the Don is the grand high witch of weaving bullshit. He'll know how to fix this."

"Are you sure?"

"Well. Have you ever been arrested?"

"What? No!"

"Then hey, your prints won't be in the system! They won't be able to ID you right away."

"I feel so much better already."

Dash was being sarcastic, of course.

He didn't feel better. In fact, he felt worse.

He'd put the entire Melvin Dashiell Purvis legacy at risk and for what? The hot guy he met at the club?

Okay, hot guy was also a member of a powerful crime family and hopefully this was all going to work out just fine, but what if it didn't?

Dash was confident he'd cleaned Darcey's house and Tommy's dad's so that there was no trace of his presence left behind, but he didn't even have a chance to at Tommy's apartment. The cops were going to find his fingerprints, maybe his hair or some trace fibers from his suit, and then there would be questions—lots of them.

Then again, Dash wasn't in the system so it wasn't like the cops would have anything to match him to...

Unless the cops got his license plate from his car in the security footage and came to the address on his registration.

Shit.

Yup. His life was ruined. There was never going to be another Melvin Purvis ever again. He was going to go to jail forever. This was the end. Maybe he'd get lucky and he and Tommy would wind up at the same prison while serving life sentences for the rest of eternity so at least he'd finally get some—

"Hey," Tommy said suddenly. "Expecting company?"

"What?" Dash blinked, hitting the brakes and snapping out of his thoughts. He'd driven home mostly on autopilot, and he was about to take the last turn onto his street. He was stopped now at the stop sign at the corner, straining to make out what Tommy was pointing at.

"Look," Tommy said. "I'm going to assume those aren't friends of yours."

There were two black SUVs parked outside Dash's place, right up on the sidewalk.

"Shit." Dash's heart sank.

"Guess my uncle isn't as stupid as I thought." Tommy scowled. "He definitely knows you're helping me now."

"Great. Wonderful. Super."

"So. Hotel?"

"Hotel."

CHAPTER 6

THE BUDGET HOST Motel was cheap, clean, and far enough away from the city limits that Dash felt safe.

Well, safe as anyone could with very angry mobsters after them anyway.

Safe-*ish*.

Dash didn't stop glancing over his shoulder until he and Tommy were safely checked into their room. He locked the door, put on the chain, and then dragged one of the side tables over to push in front of it.

"Who's Jonah Jones?" Tommy asked.

"What?" Dash turned around, not having heard him clearly. "Sorry, my ears are still kinda ringing."

Tommy had parked himself in the middle of the king-sized bed, using a washcloth from the bathroom to nurse his busted nose. "Who is Jonah?"

"Me." Dash sighed. "That's my real name."

"Jonah? Like Jonah and the fuckin' whale?"

"Yeah, well. Your ego is roughly whale-sized, isn't it?"

Tommy laughed, though judging by how he cringed after, he regretted it.

"Do you want me to get you some ice?" Dash asked, coming over to sit on the edge of the mattress.

"Nah." Tommy glanced at the door. "You worked so hard on your lil' fort or whatever it is you got going on over there."

"Shut up. I just don't want anybody else breaking in."

"Technically, those guys didn't break in because you opened the door for them—"

"Fuck off!" Dash groaned. "The app said it was the food guy! I looked through the hole! I saw food!"

"Next time someone knocks, how about you let me open it?" Tommy winked.

"Fine."

"Stick to what you're good at. Being sexy, making me laugh..."

"If you say anything about being a maid, your eye is gonna match your nose."

Tommy grinned. "I love how spicy you are. What about a maid outfit?"

"Not lookin' good for your eye."

"Hey, once I get my mind set on somethin' I want, I don't stop until I get it." Tommy's eyes widened. "Oh! Shit!"

"What now?"

"I left my dad on the counter."

"Oh." Dash frowned. "Well, I'm sure we'll be able to figure out a way to go back and get him later?"

"Damn. Yeah." Tommy frowned, his usual jovial attitude dampened. "This is some shit, huh?"

"I'll fuckin' say." Dash laid his hand on top of Tommy's. "What are we thinking? They tapped my phone or something? Found out about the order?"

"More likely they were already there watching my apartment and just happened to see the delivery guy with the food. Hell, we don't even know if that was our order. They could have just done that shit so we'd open the door."

"I'm still hungry," Dash grumbled.

"How about we try good ol' fashioned pizza delivery, huh?" Tommy laced his fingers with Dash's.

"Yeah?" Dash smiled. "Me, you, and some pizza?"

"Like that date I wanted to have with you. Maybe we'll get lucky and catch an *Ancient Aliens* marathon, huh?"

"Maybe." Dash's smile grew as Tommy closed the distance between them for a kiss. He kissed back gently, being mindful of Tommy's nose, and he let himself be drawn into Tommy's arms as the kiss rose to a steamy simmer.

This was the only thing that seemed to make any damn sense right now. Even though it was the least important item on the very long list of priorities, it was the only one Dash knew he could actually do with some success. It was easy, it was hot, and—

Dash's phone rang.

"Shit." Dash scrambled to dig into his pockets.

It was his work phone ringing.

He didn't recognize the number and thrust it at Tommy to answer. "The Don?"

"Yeah. Hagen." Tommy picked up, pushing the

speaker button. "Hello? Tommy's Ice Cream Parlor. We got thirty-two flavors of what the fuck took you so long to call me back?"

"My apologies," Hagen said. It sounded like he was rolling his eyes. "The Don has been briefed of the ongoing situation and wants to see you."

"Great! When?"

"Tomorrow morning."

"What? Why not today?"

"Why is your apartment all over the news right now?"

Tommy clicked his tongue. "Because it's a fabulous new development full of wonderful luxury accommodations?"

"Idiot!" Hagen spat. "The police identified those men as employees of your uncle. The heat is on the whole family right now. The Don wants you to stay put, and he's called your uncle to tell him to stand down."

"Yeah, and how did that go?"

"Don't worry about it." Hagen scoffed. "All you need to know is to be at the Don's house tomorrow morning at ten o'clock sharp. He'll see you then. He wants to talk to both of you before he makes a decision. Whatever proof you have, you'd better bring it."

"What about protection, huh? I'm gettin' a lil' tired of being shot at today. I don't want this to be a habit."

"The Don already called for a ceasefire. If you want more than that, I have to know where you are first."

Tommy hesitated, and his brow furrowed. He glanced to Dash.

Dash shrugged helplessly. He gestured to the table in front of the door.

"Nah, I'm all right, Hagen." Tommy scrubbed his hand over his face. "I'm good for now."

"See you tomorrow, bright-eyed and bushy-tailed."

"The fuck does that even mean?"

"It means be ready and bring the fuckin' proof with you."

"Got it." Tommy hung up and then sighed loudly. "Well, I think that went okay."

"Why didn't you tell him where we were?" Dash asked. "I thought you wanted protection."

"Because I'm feeling like a paranoid motherfucker all of a sudden." Tommy flopped back in bed. "It's probably nothing, but we didn't get attacked until after I talked to Hagen."

"Well, hiding at your own apartment isn't exactly sneaky," Dash pointed out. "It's a good first place to look. Your uncle definitely knows you're alive now, right? Since the Don called him?"

"Yeah. He's either ignoring the Don's orders or the Don didn't talk to him until after he had already sent those assholes to take another swipe at me." Tommy nudged Dash. "And you."

Dash cringed. "I hate to think what the fuck they've done to my apartment."

"Try not to. Besides, I know a great maid."

Dash pushed Tommy's arm.

"Hey! I meant a real maid!" Tommy laughed. "Like, you know, a cleaning service of the not dead body variety!" He swatted at Dash's hip. "You don't have the right kind of uniform."

"Maybe I do," Dash teased.

"I've been in your closet. I would have found it."

"Right, because that's where I would keep my sexy maid outfit."

Tommy's brow furrowed, and then he grinned. "I can't tell if you're fucking with me, but now all I'm thinking about is you as a sexy maid and I am so turned the fuck on."

"Food," Dash said firmly. "We're ordering food. I am starving."

"What do you want? Extra large meat lovers?"

"Ugh."

Dash preferred plain cheese, and Tommy got a pepperoni and two two-liters of soda. Tommy also promised the delivery person a huge tip if he got them a bottle of whiskey. Dash helped Tommy move the table when there was a knock at the door, but he let Tommy open it this time.

Tommy had a gun tucked in the back of his pants, but he was all smiles as he tipped the young delivery woman two crisp hundred dollar bills for bringing the booze.

Dash opted for regular soda with dinner, and he noted Tommy's hand was a bit heavy when he added whiskey to his. Tommy lamented that his stomach was going to hate him for this later, but he deserved to have pizza. They ate while Tommy scrolled through channels on the TV, and he laughed when he found it:

An *Ancient Aliens* marathon on the History Channel.

"Guess we got that romantic date after all," Tommy teased.

Dash chuckled. "And you didn't even have to pirate anything."

"Boo."

"I'd say it's still pretty nice, all things considered." Dash shrugged. "Hey, I'm out of the house." He cringed. "And I just remembered I have three fucking cremations that I rescheduled for tomorrow... that I will now have to reschedule *again*."

"Is that bad?"

"Well, if they need the ashes ready by a certain date for the funeral, yeah, it's bad. They'll take their business elsewhere."

"You mean the bodies."

"Yeah."

"Don't you have somebody you can call in to help you?" Tommy frowned. "Or is it really just you?"

"Just me and my handy dandy hydraulic lift. Heh. Kinda can't have anybody helping me because they might start asking questions."

"About your, uh, concrete mix?" Tommy sipped his drink. He'd slowed down on the alcohol, though his easy smile suggested he was already pretty buzzed.

"Exactly."

They were sitting in bed against the headboard, their respective pizza boxes beside them. Dash had eaten half of his while Tommy had devoured the entire pie. Now that he had something on his stomach, Dash accepted Tommy's offer to share the whiskey, but he had to stop him from adding too much.

"You really like your drinks crunchy, huh?" Dash chuckled.

"It's been a hell of a day." Tommy raised his plastic cup in a toast.

"That it has." Dash bumped his cup against Tommy's.

"I deserve all the pizza and booze."

"You damn sure do. You were pretty bad ass."

"I was, huh?" Tommy winked. "I know, I know. I'm pretty fuckin' awesome."

"Where did you learn to fight like that?"

"I dunno." Tommy finished his cup, but he set it aside instead of refilling it. "Got into a lot of scraps when I was a kid. Shit was rough for a little while. But I won more fights than I lost, so my dad eventually started sending me around to help encourage guys to pay up when shit was due."

"Sounds... fun."

"It's a job. Do what you gotta do and all that."

"It's more than that though, right? Because it's your family?"

"I'm not really feelin' the family love right this second." Tommy grimaced. "My dad's wake is gonna be real fuckin' awkward."

"We still need proof, right?" Dash slurped at his drink. "That your uncle was stealing money and tried to kill you?"

"Well, you're kinda my proof, I guess. You got called to the damn house to clean up our damn corpses and shit. You can tell the Don that much, right?"

"Yeah, but an anonymous text message doesn't

exactly scream, *hey, my name is Dio Capelli and I did it.*"
Dash shivered as Tommy's hand slid over his thigh. "We
need more than that."

"I need an orgasm. It helps me think."

"Really?" Dash's cock twitched in his pants, and he
watched Tommy's hand move higher.

"Yup, sure does." Tommy leaned over to mouth at
Dash's throat. "Mmm, I'm only trying to do what's best
for us."

"Us, huh?" Dash closed his eyes, savoring the scratch
of Tommy's scruff. Tommy's fingers had reached his
crotch but only teased his inner thigh, not yet touching
his cock.

"Mm-hmm." Tommy chuckled. "For as long as you
can stand the sheer awesomeness of my incredible
company."

"Sure there's enough room for me with your ego?"

"Oh, I'll make sure it fits," Tommy teased.

"Mm, one sec." Dash turned to put his drink and then
his glasses on the bedside table. He surged back into
Tommy's waiting arms, kissing him hard.

Tommy easily moved on top of Dash, pinning him to
the bed with his hips as they kissed. He slotted his hard
dick against Dash's and slid his hand underneath Dash's
shirt, pushing his tongue slowly into Dash's mouth.

Dash hugged Tommy's broad shoulders, already in
love with the warmth of his body pressing against his
own. He even liked the faint clink of Tommy's tongue
ring grazing his teeth. He shifted so his legs were
squeezing Tommy's hips, and he tangled his hands in
Tommy's hair.

Tommy rocked his hips slowly, putting the perfect amount of pressure on their cocks. His kisses were deep, passionate, and stole Dash's breath away.

Dash couldn't remember the last time he'd kissed someone like this—long presses of lips, hot slides of tongue, and firm rolls of their bodies grinding together. He ran his hands down over Tommy's neck, holding him there to devour his mouth and push their erections together more insistently.

The temperature in the room was rising, and Dash's brow was already prickling with sweat from their steamy kiss. He tugged at Tommy's shirt, and he mumbled, "Do you have, uh, well, anything?"

"Yeah, I got lube."

"What? Like one of those little wallet packs?"

"Maybe I told the pizza girl to bring some." Tommy chuckled breathlessly.

"Seriously?" Dash pushed at Tommy's chest. "You were *that* sure we were gonna have sex?"

"I mean..." Tommy grinned. "Yes?"

Dash laughed. "You are an ass." He kissed him.

"Mmm, and I'm about to get all up in your ass, baby."

"Get the lube, Tommy."

"Sir, yes, sir!" Tommy reared back on his knees, and then he leaned over to grab the paper bag the booze had come in. He reached in and pulled out a new bottle of lubricant.

Dash had his shirt off by the time Tommy had the plastic peeled from the cap, but Tommy clicked his tongue when Dash went for his pants.

"Slowly, slowly," Tommy soothed. "Hang on a second."

"What?"

"Allow me." Tommy dropped the lube on the bed as he crawled between Dash's thighs. He paused only to remove his shirt and jacket, humming as he did so and wagging his hips.

Dash's heart pounded faster, and he drank in the enticing display as he got settled in the pillows. He tried to sit up and reach for Tommy, but Tommy pushed him back down. "Hey, what gives?"

"Just showing you some gratitude," Tommy replied, his hand fanning over Dash's chest. "You did save my life, you know." He kissed the line of Dash's collarbone. "Mmm, and I am so very, very grateful."

"Yeah?" Dash panted, and his cock was now tenting the front of his pants. "All right then. So show me."

"Gladly." Tommy ghosted his lips down Dash's chest, pausing to suck on his nipples. He gave each one firm sucks and hungry kisses, and then he moved down Dash's stomach. He grabbed the waistband of his pants with his teeth, his eyes flicking up to meet Dash's.

He was looking at Dash as if he was the most desirable creature in all of the universe, and Dash's loins clenched up so tightly that he thought he might come.

Tommy used his teeth and fingers to unbuckle Dash's belt, and his eyes gleamed with the excitement of someone about to open a shiny present. He mouthed along Dash's cock through his pants as he pulled his zipper, groaning low.

Dash dug his hands into Tommy's hair, urging him to keep going. "Fuck, come on."

"Mmm, my pretty maid is impatient." Tommy pushed open the fly of Dash's pants.

"Pretty maid can hide your body."

"Oh, I know you can, and it's one of my favorite things about you." Tommy scooted back to give himself enough room to pull Dash's pants and underwear off. He threw them over his shoulder and then dove back in, lying flat on his stomach so he could wiggle back in position between Dash's legs.

The anticipation was thick, heavy, and Dash's cock was dancing with his rapid pulse.

Tommy kissed the crease of Dash's groin, and he pushed at his inner thigh. "Spread 'em, babe."

Dash yanked his legs apart so quickly that he kicked off one of the pizza boxes, and he didn't even care because Tommy's tongue was right there, lapping at his asshole.

"Mmph, *baby*." Tommy licked up and down, his fingers greedily kneading at the underside of Dash's thighs. He moved his thumbs inward to probe around Dash's hole, and he focused the tip of his tongue there, probing relentlessly.

Dash closed his eyes and basked in the awesome pleasure, and he gave Tommy's hair a tug. "God, yeah. That feels so fuckin' good."

"Not too shabby, eh?" Tommy quipped.

"Not bad for an accountant." Dash gasped when Tommy lightly jabbed his hole with the tip of his thumb. "Mm, hey!"

"This accountant is about to take you to another planet, baby." Tommy chuckled, withdrawing so his tongue could get back to work.

"Mmm, let's go." Dash groaned, his asshole getting soft and wet from Tommy's determined tongue. He didn't feel the piercing as much as he thought he would, but it was still exciting and new. When Tommy's thumb came again to tease him, it slipped in easily, and he savored the stretch. He heard the lube cap clicking open, and he welcomed the new ease the lubricant allowed so Tommy could push his thumb in deeper.

Tommy licked a stripe up to Dash's balls, and he winked right before he sucked one into his mouth.

Dash's cock was dripping precome now, and he groaned as Tommy replaced his thumb with one of his fingers so he could press deeper and coax out a few whimpers. He petted Tommy's hair encouragingly, and he rocked down on his hand.

Tommy hummed, switching to Dash's other ball to suck around it as he fingered him. He thrust gently, twisting a little as he pulled out, and he kissed the base of Dash's cock. "Can you imagine me doing this..."

"What?" Dash grunted, his hips jerking as Tommy pressed in a second finger.

"Under the skirt of your sexy little maid outfit?"

Dash laughed. He couldn't help it, though the sound morphed into a groan as Tommy's fingers moved just right. "You... and that damn maid outfit."

"Told you before." Tommy thrust faster. "When I get my mind on somethin' I want, I get it. I wanted you from the second I saw you at that damn bar."

"And now you want me in a maid outfit?" Dash laughed again, smiling down at Tommy.

"I want you in a thousand different ways, baby." Tommy grinned. "I can't wait to try 'em all."

Dash squeezed around Tommy's fingers as he grinded down on his hand again. "Come on then. Let's try door number one, sex in a hotel room."

"You got it, baby." Tommy slid his fingers out and then brushed his thumb over Dash's asshole. "Mm, you ready for me?"

Dash's lashes fluttered, and he nodded. He was hot and tingling all over, and his hole was aching for something to fill it. "Yeah, but I..."

"What is it?" Tommy sat back on his heels as he undid his belt and pants.

"I've never fucked anyone who had their dick pierced before."

"Well, good news." Tommy wiggled out of his clothes, kicking them off with a grin. "If you don't like it, I can take it out."

"Really?"

"Yeah, the bead just pops out. No biggie."

Dash stared at Tommy's cock as he lubed himself up. Tommy's dick was beautiful and Dash couldn't wait to have every inch of it, but the ring was suddenly intimidating knowing that it was supposed to go inside of him.

It was *big*.

"You want me to take it out now?" Tommy smiled. "Because you're looking at me like it's gonna bite you."

"It fuckin' might."

Tommy leaned down, propping himself on his

elbows as he moved on top of Dash. He nuzzled their noses together and said, "All you gotta do is tell me what you want, baby."

Dash shivered. "I think today has already been exciting enough."

"Done and done, baby."

"It won't close up, will it?"

"Nah, I've had this a long time. It's fine. Especially with a gauge this big, it's not going anywhere." Tommy fumbled with the ring. "Kinda wish I'd done this before covering my dick with lube, but hey, hindsight is—"

Something blipped across Dash's vision, and there was a distinctly metallic *ping* from the far corner of the room. "What was that?"

"Uh, that would be the ball to my dick ring that just popped out."

"Shit! Do we, uh, need to go get it?"

"Later." Tommy pounced on top of Dash. "The only thing I wanna get right now is that fine ass, baby. Now come on. I still got a lot of gratitude to give you."

Dash dragged his fingers over Tommy's chest, hitching his legs on Tommy's hips as he kissed him. "Mm, yeah, I suddenly feel the need to be appreciated very thoroughly."

"Oh, and you will be, I guarantee it." Tommy pressed his cock to Dash's ass, watching intently as he slid the head in. "Mmm, there we go, baby."

Dash breathed in and smiled, savoring the first taste of penetration. It had been quite some time for him, and he'd missed that hot stretch. "Fuck, feels good."

"Yeah?" Tommy pushed in more, and his eyes shifted to watch Dash's face. "You like that?"

"Mmhmm." Dash palmed Tommy's pecs, squeezing hungrily. "This is all I want. Just you."

"You got it, baby." Tommy kissed him, and he groaned when Dash pinched his nipples. He thrust steadily, working himself in a little deeper each time, and he slid a hand down to grab Dash's thigh.

Dash loved the strong grip of Tommy's fingers, and the relentless press of his cock was fantastic. The pleasure was building fast from the sensual roll of Tommy's hips, and Dash let himself enjoy every sweet second of it. He was really getting into it now, but he was surprised when Tommy suddenly grinned down at him. "Wh-what is it?"

"You're so fuckin' hot." Tommy kissed him. "And Christ, you feel so fuckin' good."

"You too." Dash blushed. "God, you too."

Tommy kissed him again, and they both groaned when Tommy was finally fully seated inside of him.

Dash's hole throbbed, and he whined against Tommy's lips, rocking his body down to encourage him to continue. He didn't understand what Tommy was waiting for. "Come on."

"Easy, easy." Tommy nosed Dash's cheek. "Just savoring the moment, baby. You feel amazing."

"Gonna feel even better if you actually *move*."

Tommy gave Dash a playful slam.

"*Mm*, there we go."

Tommy teased his cock in and out with slow slides, giving Dash's thigh another squeeze. His entire body moved as he fucked him, his back arching as he pushed his hips forward, and he mouthed over Dash's jaw and throat.

Dash closed his eyes as zings of sensation rippled through him. The friction of Tommy's cock sliding inside of him was perfect, just enough to make him grunt, and Tommy's breath against his throat made him shudder and got his nipples hard.

Tommy seemed sure Dash could take more now because he pounded into him faster, and Dash groaned happily. It was amazing, and he had missed how good it felt to be this full. Tommy read his body language perfectly and was hitting all the right nerves that made Dash's toes curl. He wanted more, and he pulled his legs up until his knees were in his chest, grabbing a handful of Tommy's ass.

"You like that, baby?" Tommy purred. "Mmm, feelin' good?"

"Yeah. I wanna come," Dash pleaded. "Come on."

"Are you close?" Tommy fucked him faster.

"Yeah, you?"

"Fuck yes."

"Come on then. Give it to me." Dash gritted his teeth, grabbing his dick as he arched his hips. He knew it was going to be fast, but he didn't care. Tommy was fucking him down into the mattress like a damn machine now, and Dash was too worked up to be concerned with how loudly he was moaning or how the bed was slamming into the wall.

Tommy's merciless drilling was tempered by the tender caress of his hands along Dash's thighs and the soft press of his lips to Dash's throat as he urged, "Come on, baby. Come on, bust for me. I wanna feel you comin' on my dick."

"Don't stop, don't stop." Dash grunted. "Even if you fuckin' come, don't you dare fuckin' stop!" He jerked himself faster, his hand a blur on his dick as he tried to push himself over the edge. Their bodies were crashing together so fast now that it sounded like someone clapping, and the frantic friction dragged the most sinful cries from Dash's throat. The pressure was ticking up and up, and he gasped as it finally gave way to an explosive orgasm.

He clenched around Tommy's cock, twitching as he shot his load between them. His chest heaved, and he groaned when he felt Tommy swell inside of him. The rush of hot come only added to his pleasure, and he grinded down to meet Tommy for the final few slams of their climaxes. He swore the room went fuzzy and it wasn't only because he didn't have his glasses on.

Tommaso Capelli had thoroughly fucked his brains out and clearly it was affecting his vision.

Tommy let out a few very satisfied groans as he slid his cock in and out, playing in the slick slide his come had created. He pressed a breathless kiss to Dash's lips, mumbling, "Fuck, that was awesome, baby. Oh, my *fuck*."

Dash grinned dopily. "It sure was, huh?"

"Do you feel appreciated?" Tommy batted his lashes.

Dash laughed, looping one of his arms over Tommy's shoulders. He kissed him, tender and deep, and then he bucked down on Tommy's cock. "Fuck yeah."

"Mmph!" Tommy grunted, clearly too sensitive as he

withdrew from Dash's body with a sharp gasp. "Mm, you mean, mean man."

"Sorry."

"You don't sound very sorry."

"Probably because I'm not." Dash cackled as he dragged Tommy back in for another kiss. He was warm, heavy all over, and he couldn't stop smiling. He hooked a leg around Tommy's hips to keep him close, content to keep making out until necessity called for a towel to clean up the mess.

Tommy went to get it, springing away to the bathroom with an extra pep in his step.

Alone for the moment, Dash sprawled across the bed and enjoyed the lingering throb between his legs from being so freshly fucked. His heartbeat was slowing down now, and he stretched his body out, grunting as a few joints popped. A few of his muscles were sore in funny places, probably from lack of use, and he made a mental note to stretch more.

It hadn't been something he worried about much since his love life had been about as lively as the people he cremated, but now...

Dash's heart fluttered when Tommy joined him in bed again, and he thought that he might have a reason to.

"Assume the position, sir," Tommy said in a firm voice.

"Oh, right away." Dash laughed and spread his legs so Tommy could wipe him down. "And he even got the water warm. What a gentleman."

"I'm the full package, baby." Tommy winked.

"Beauty, brains, and…" His eyes widened. "Holy fuck. I know where to get the proof!"

"Seriously?" Dash blinked.

"Yeah!"

"Wow. Maybe coming really does help you think."

"I mean, we could go again just to make sure—"

"No. Come on. Wherever this proof is, we need to go get it fuckin' yesterday."

"Sure, just one quick thing."

"What?"

"Gotta find the ball for my dick ring."

CHAPTER 7

AFTER FINDING THE MISSING BALL, they quickly got dressed. Dash was curious about how exactly Tommy got the jewelry in, but that was a mystery for another time. He was more interested in knowing what proof had been magically revealed to Tommy by the power of an orgasm.

"Okay, so." Tommy was sitting on the edge of the bed, putting his socks and shoes back on. "I was wearing that wire from Darcey for like the last two weeks, okay? Running around the cash houses and trying to get something on Dio, right?"

"Okay?" Dash frowned. "But you said yourself that you guys hadn't found anything."

"Yeah, but that night when I called Darcey to tell him Dio was after me?" Tommy stood. "I told him we were fucked, and he says no, that he found somethin' using one of the recordings. Somethin' to do with one of the banks and that we were gonna be fine. I forgot about it until just right fuckin' now." He grinned. "See? Orgasms really do help."

"But he didn't tell you what it was?"

"No, he just told me to haul ass on over there." Tommy appeared thoughtful. "Maybe we've been thinkin' about this all wrong."

"How do you mean?"

"Maybe Dio isn't out to get me because of the wire. Maybe he's trying to fuckin' kill me because of something Darcey found."

Dash's brow furrowed. "Yeah, but how would he know Darcey had something?"

"Well..." Tommy frowned. "Okay, I dunno, but what I do know is that Darcey's place is the only damn place that might have what we need. Plus, Dio and them probably won't come looking for us there."

"Except you just theorized Dio knew about Darcey's evidence, which gives him a great reason to go there looking to destroy it."

"You are no fun."

"Fun is not exactly what I would describe this as."

"Hey." Tommy eyed Dash hungrily. "Some of it has been *real* fun."

Dash ducked his head. "Let's go."

They left the motel, and Dash drove them over to Darcey's. He was expecting to see more big black cars waiting for them, but the driveway was empty. He and Tommy hurried to the front door, and Tommy drew back his elbow as if he was about to smash the glass next to the door.

"Wait, wait!" Dash hissed.

"What?"

Dash kneeled and lifted the doormat, revealing the key.

"Oh, that works too."

Dash put on a pair of latex gloves before he picked up the key.

"You just carry those around with you?" Tommy teased.

"Keep them in my glove box." Dash unlocked the door.

"What, I don't get any?"

"You knew Darcey. It wouldn't be strange for someone to find your prints here." Dash quickly ushered Tommy inside and then shut the door behind him.

"Okay, fine." Tommy rolled his eyes. "Keep all your cool gloves to yourself."

Dash had never returned to a place he'd cleaned before, and he felt a little anxious—especially standing a few feet away from where Tommy's father had died.

Hopefully Tommy wouldn't notice.

And he didn't, of course. The contractors had done their work well, and there was no sign that blood had ever been spilled here.

Tommy headed back into the main bedroom, stopping short at the doorway.

"What's wrong?" Dash asked him.

"Damn." Tommy laughed. "You really do good work, maid. It looks crazy nice in here."

"Thank you. Now how about you be a good accountant and find some bank transfers or whatever."

"Fine, fine. Come on." Tommy continued down the

hall to another bedroom with built-in bookshelves lining the wall. He pulled the books out from the bottom shelf and pressed the side, opening a hidden compartment. From inside, he pulled out a big black briefcase. "Ta-dah!"

"How the hell did you know that was there?"

"Darcey and my dad grew up together, remember? He told me about this spot. It's where they used to hide their weed and girly mags." Tommy tapped the top of the briefcase. "Let's see what we got."

Dash half-expected the damn thing to be empty.

Tommy opened it, revealing a thick stack of papers, a few folders, and a dozen small cassette tapes. Right on top was a handwritten letter, and Tommy read it out loud. "Leo, I'm sorry I don't have time to explain, but this is everything you need. Get the bastard." He made a face. "*Fuck.*"

"Darcey must have called your dad?" Dash said quietly.

"Yeah, I guess he was the backup Darcey was talkin' about. Had to be. I don't think anybody else knew about this hiding spot. Not even my fuckin' uncle." Tommy grabbed the paperwork, handing off a folder to Dash. "Here, have some light reading."

"Goody." Dash flipped through the folder, finding it contained transcripts, presumably from Tommy's time wearing the wire. There were notes on the sides written in the same scratchy handwriting as the letter, and the only thing Dash could make out was FFCU written in all caps.

"Huh." Tommy frowned at the papers and stood to show them to Dash. "Look at this."

"What is it?"

"Bank statements, but it's not any account I've ever seen. We don't have any with First Federal. None that I know of anyway."

"Who's Williams Vigars? That's the name."

"No clue. Probably a dummy. Like a fake account." Tommy pointed to a few transactions. "See? The same amount that's deposited gets transferred out a few days later."

Dash whistled at all the zeros. "That's a big amount."

"Yup."

"Hang on a second." Dash glanced at the transcript. "FFCU, First Federal Credit Union."

"That's Darcey's handwriting," Tommy noted.

"The transcript is... Well, you were talking about having, uh, some stomach issues." Dash chuckled.

"Hey, not having a gallbladder sucks." Tommy scowled. "And speaking of which, I'll be right back."

"Good luck."

Tommy left for the bathroom, and Dash kept reading.

While Tommy was complaining of his intestinal issues in great detail, Dio had apparently been on the phone and his side of the conversation had been picked up by the wire.

DIO: No, that's the fuckin' wrong routing number. What's that? Three two six? Four three two six? No, that's not right.

Dash assumed that Darcey had used that to narrow down banks until he found the account at First Federal.

He had no idea what criteria Darcey used to identify this particular account or how he'd gotten access, but the printed statements were from the same one.

He paused on a page where some of the transfers were highlighted, and he read over the amounts a few times. There was a note at the top of the page with what he assumed was another account number, but he focused instead on the transactions. He wasn't the best at math in the world, but he definitely knew when something didn't add up.

"Hey!" Tommy was back. "Find something?"

"I think so." Dash handed the paper to Tommy.

"What's this?"

"If I'm reading it correctly, I think it's your missing money," Dash replied. "You said the deposits always get transferred out, right? But look at those. Ten thousand went in, six thousand went out, and four thousand was written as a check cashed the very next day. Same with the twenty thousand. Two checks that time, but the full amount definitely did not get transferred."

Tommy's brow wrinkled. "That can't be right. I mean, yeah, sometimes we might split up payments, but we would never write a fuckin' check like this."

"So, this is it. Darcey found the account and the missing money."

"Would have been real nice of him to fuckin' tell me who it belonged to."

"You don't know who this Vigars guy is, right?"

"Never heard of him."

"Shit. I don't understand why he didn't just say who the bastard was in his note. There has to be something here that we're missing, something that could clue your father in to who it was..."

Tommy grimaced. "Well, as soon as I see it, I'll let you know."

"Hang on a sec." Dash scanned the account number. "It might just..." He grabbed his phone to check his banking app. "Fuck."

"What?"

"I can only see the last four of the account number that paid me to clean the house, but look. Now look at the account number written up here on the top of the page."

"Holy fuck. It's the same. And that number? It's one of the family's accounts. My uncle controls that one." Tommy gasped. "My dad would totally recognize that number. That must be what Darcey left for him to see. This printed shit must belong to some bogus account my uncle's been sifting the money through! This is it!" He kissed Dash hard. "Fuck yeah!"

"Well." Dash adjusted his glasses. "We still don't know for sure whose account all this paperwork is for. Darcey just wrote a number, not a name."

"But that account number is totally Dio's. William whoever is just some stupid name he made up to cover his ass." Tommy snorted. "All that matters is I have fuckin' proof to bring the Don tomorrow. Come on." He packed the papers back into the briefcase. "Let's get the fuck outta here."

"Back to the hotel?"

"Yeah." Tommy flashed a cheeky grin.

"Can you drive? I still have to reschedule my cremations and it's not gonna be very pleasant."

"Sure thing, baby. Unless... Do you wanna run back over there right now? Fire up the barbeque?"

"If your uncle's men already figured out where I live, they're probably watching the crematory too." Dash cringed. "I am gonna have to cancel the cremations completely and send the funeral homes over to my competitor."

"Well, I'll make sure my uncle fuckin' pays for that too."

"It's all right." Dash winked. "I'm doing pretty okay."

"Right." Tommy smirked. "Since you got paid for this big cleaning job."

"It was pretty big."

"I'm glad it was such a profitable experience for you."

"The best." Dash led the way out the front door. He put the key back under the mat and then they headed to the hotel. Tommy drove so Dash could make the necessary and grueling phone calls.

By the time they got back to the hotel, he'd already lost the funeral home with the very frazzled funeral director permanently and pissed off the other two.

Wonderful.

Dash was glad there was still whiskey left.

Back inside their room, Dash returned the table to its spot in front of the door and asked, "Could you make me a drink?"

"That bad, huh?" Tommy cringed.

"It definitely was not good."

"Crunchy?"

"I wanna be able to chew it."

"Can do, baby."

Dash groaned as he walked over to the bed. He flopped right in the middle with a defeated grunt. "That fuckin' sucked."

"Well, it could be worse," Tommy said cheerfully as he poured.

"How?"

"They could have tried to kill you."

"Fair." Dash took off his glasses so he could rub the bridge of his nose. "The funeral business can be pretty nasty, but at least I don't have to worry about someone whacking me."

"Rub it in, why don't you?" Tommy handed Dash a cup. "Here."

"Thank you." Dash took a sip and immediately hissed. It tasted like pure whiskey.

Tommy chuckled. "Crunchy enough for you?"

"Perfect."

Tommy had made a drink for himself and he climbed in bed beside Dash. "So. Gettin' hungry?"

"Not yet. Still have some pizza left. How's your stomach?"

"Probably need to eat something green and not fried. Kinda wrecked to be honest, but it turns out that I'm also a tiny bit stressed."

"Can't imagine why."

"Right?" Tommy laughed.

"Is that normal after gallbladder surgery? Getting, you know..."

"The shits?" Tommy replied bluntly. "Yeah, it's a pretty common side effect. Can last a few weeks or a few months, and I'm the lucky bastard who's had it now goin' on for four fuckin' months."

"Ouch."

Tommy slurped at his drink. "Hey, it's all right. It's makin' me eat healthier. Cut back on my drinking."

"Really?" Dash eyed Tommy's cup, already half-empty. "Cutting back, huh?"

"I've had a lot of people trying to kill me today. Don't judge me."

Dash took Tommy's hand. "Nah, I'm just messing with you."

"You can mess with me all you want after I've had a shower." Tommy squeezed Dash's hand in reply. "Or in the shower if you'd like."

"I'm okay right now." Dash chuckled and then took a sip of his drink. "Trying to figure out what we can order for dinner."

"I'm trying to figure out how to get you into that bathroom with me."

"Again with the bathroom?"

"I just wanna go again with you."

Dash laughed. "Come on. Down, boy."

"I'll go down—"

Dash let go of Tommy's hand so he could bop his chest. "Easy, easy! God, you're like one giant hormone."

"It's at least forty percent of my personality."

"Go take your shower and think about what you want to eat for dinner. And don't say my ass."

"Fine." Tommy kissed Dash's cheek. "I'm going, but I'll be touching myself and thinking about you very soon."

"You're so romantic."

Tommy winked as he slid off the bed, taking his drink with him to the bathroom.

Alone now, Dash sagged into the mattress. He was warm from the whiskey, and it helped soothe the cringe of recalling the chats with the funeral homes. His reputation was very important, and he knew it would take some time to recover from this damage.

Beat the hell out of being dead though.

Dash's phone rang, his personal phone, and he grimaced when he saw who it was.

It was Mel.

His mentor, friend, and absolutely the last person he wanted to talk to right now.

Shit.

He didn't want Mel to know what he'd gotten mixed up in. He'd broken their one rule of not interfering with the living repeatedly, and he was literally on the run for his life because some of the Capelli family wanted him dead.

Dash let the call go to voicemail, but he didn't have long to be relieved because the phone rang again.

Shit.

Dash answered, "Hello?"

"Heya, kiddo," Mel's gravelly voice rumbled through the line. "You got a second?"

"Uh, well—"

"Because I'd like to know why I got a call from Hall Blake askin' why my *son* is letting the crematory go to fuckin' shit."

Dash cringed and tipped his cup back again.

"Well?" Mel pressed. "Is it true? You had to blow off a fuckin' cremation?"

"Uh, well, there were three—"

"*Three*?"

"I had some technical difficulties—"

"Why didn't you fuckin' call me, huh?" Mel growled. "I could have driven up there if it was that damn bad! I can still run that dragon, you know."

"Right, but—"

"You know how vital it is to keep that damn crematory in good standing. It's the backbone of the whole business. It's how we do what the fuck we do, okay? It's the key to fuckin' everything!"

Dash kept drinking as Mel raged on, wishing that the alcohol would somehow transmit through the line and chill Mel out for a moment. When that didn't seem to be working, he finally blurted out, "Look, I had a problem with a job, and I needed time to handle it, okay?"

"What kinda fuckin' problem?" Mel demanded. "You leave somethin' behind? Somebody see you?"

"No, nothing like that."

"Then what?"

Dash's head swam, and he replied weakly, "There was an issue with a problem not being a problem."

"*What*?" Mel's voice rose to a shout.

Dash had to pull the phone away from his ear, but he could still hear Mel clearly as he raged.

"Someone was still fucking *alive*? Jesus fuckin' *Christ*, Dash! What did you do? Huh? Did you call the client back? Please don't fuckin' tell me you tried to help—"

"Okay, then I won't tell you."

"You dumbass!" Mel groaned in frustration. "What the fuck happened?"

"Fuck!" Dash's gut clenched, and he finished off the drink. "Right. So. There were five problems, but I was only paid for four. One of them was maybe a guy I'd met at a really fancy club, and... well..."

"Who the fuck is it?"

"Tommaso Capelli."

"Leonardo's kid?" Mel groaned loudly.

"Yes, and uh, Leonardo is sort of dead? He was the mystery number five, and apparently Dio, his brother, might be stealing money from the family. He's been trying to kill us, and now we're going to see the Don tomorrow—"

"Who the fuck is *we*?"

"Me and Tommy."

"*Tommy*, huh?" Mel scoffed. "All right, kiddo. Let's back up a bit. Tell me what the fuck happened, from the beginning."

Dash did his best to relay the exciting events, though he chose to exclude some of the details, like sleeping with Tommy and what they did on the desk in the crematory. He kept it short and concise, and he was cringing inwardly the entire time. He was preparing himself for the ass chewing of the century, and he finished by saying, "I'm sorry I let you down. I just... I needed to do the right thing."

Mel sighed—a long, haggard, and very annoyed sigh.

Dash grimaced.

"You fuckin' dumbass," Mel said at last. "You got yourself in the middle of a fuckin' mob war?"

"Uh. Possibly. Yes."

"So." Mel actually sounded like he was smiling. "You fuck Tommaso yet?"

"Fuckin' hell, Mel." Dash scrubbed his hand over his face, pushing his glasses up on his forehead. "Does that really matter?"

"Pretty sure it does since your dick is the one making stupid ass decisions," Mel replied. "If you're gonna die for some ass, you might as well be tappin' it, kid. But seriously. You need to get yourself straightened out fast. You really think this bullshit proof is gonna be enough to clean up the shit you've stepped in?"

Dash hesitated. "I think so, yeah."

"*Think* so?"

"Yeah, I'm pretty fuckin' sure!"

Tommy emerged from the bathroom wearing nothing but a smile. He strutted toward the bed, but he paused when he saw Dash on the phone. He pointed at the phone, cocking his head curiously.

Dash made a face.

"Over a hundred years of prestige and dignified problem-solving service is about to come to an end because you *think* you have what you need," Mel grumbled. "Jesus fuckin' Christ."

"I'm gonna handle it," Dash said firmly. "It's gonna be fine."

"Who are you trying to convince, kid?"

"I said I've got this, Mel."

Tommy jumped into bed, lying across Dash's lap. He batted his eyes up at him and then reached for his pants.

Dash ignored him.

At least, he tried to.

It was very difficult, however, to ignore someone unzipping his pants and grabbing his dick.

"Listen to me very carefully," Mel was saying. "The Capelli family is no joke. We've been their go-to cleaner for generations. Even if you're on the winning side, you've tainted any sense of impartiality with them, okay?"

"Right." Dash smacked at Tommy's hands, and he mumbled under his breath at him, "Not right now."

Tommy pretended like he didn't understand, miming confusion, and then he successfully freed Dash's cock. With a sly smile and no warning, he ran his tongue over the head.

Dash knew this was a losing battle, but he pushed at Tommy's shoulder, trying to resist his advances. The slick heat of Tommy's tongue and the smooth drag of the piercing were just too awesome, and there was nothing he could do to stop the rush of blood surging right to his dick.

"We are not supposed to pick sides," Mel droned on. "We clean for anybody, any damn time."

"Yup. Anybody, anytime," Dash echoed.

"Are you even listening to me?"

"Yes! I'm listen-*ing*!" Dash choked on the last syllable as Tommy sucked his dick into his mouth. He bit his lip to keep from moaning, and he glared daggers at a very smug Tommy.

Tommy swallowed him down to his balls, sucking hard and moaning much more loudly than necessary.

"I love you, kid. You're like a son to me." Mel sighed.

"You've always had a good head on your shoulders, I'd trust you with my fuckin' life, but... This is a fuckin' mess and a half."

"I know," Dash said between gritted teeth. "I know, I know."

"When do you see the Don?"

"Tomorrow. Ten."

"Are you all right? You sound kinda funny."

Tommy pushed Dash's cock into the back of his throat, and he lightly squeezed his balls.

Dash gasped. "I'm good. I'm fine." He cleared his throat, trying to sound as normal as possible as he added, "It's, uh, just been very stressful. You know, being shot at. Twice. So very stressful."

"Be careful out there, kiddo," Mel warned. "I really don't wanna come back to Old Defiance and train another me, okay? And for fuck's sake, when this shit is done? You're gonna call those funeral homes and kiss some ass. A Purvis never loses clients of any damn kind, you understand me?"

"Yup. Got it."

"Say it."

"Huh?" Dash was having trouble thinking now since Tommy was busy sucking his brains out through his cock.

"Say it so I know you understand," Mel ordered. "Tell me what you're gonna do when this shit is all handled."

"Call funeral homes. Kiss ass."

"There! Was that so fuckin' hard?"

Dash resisted the urge to laugh at the word *hard* since he was currently throbbing in Tommy's mouth, and he said quickly, "Thank you, Mel. For everything. I gotta go now, but, uh, I'll talk to you very soon."

"You'd damn well better." Mel chuckled. "Don't make me leave my nice sandy beach just to come up there and kick your ass."

"Thank you. Talk soon."

"Remember, kid. You gotta be alive to be happy."

"Yes. Alive. Happy. Bye bye now!"

"Bye—"

Dash practically threw his phone after hanging up, and then he dug his hands into Tommy's hair with a groan. "God, what the fuck are you doing? Seriously? That was a very important conversation!"

Tommy pulled off with a juicy pop. "It sounded very important and therefore very stressful. Getting a blowjob? Definitely helps with stress."

"Okay, while that may be true, you can't just... do that!"

"But it looks like I did." Tommy ran his tongue around the head of Dash's dick, focusing the ball of his piercing around the slit. "And I am. And I wasn't planning on stopping, but if you don't want me to finish..." He leaned back as if he was pulling away.

"Oh, you bastard, no!" Dash laughed, playfully grabbing Tommy's head to push him back down. "Come on now. You finish what the hell you started."

"Who was on the phone?" Tommy teased his tongue up the side of Dash's dick.

"Melvin Purvis."

"But that's you."

"Mel, my mentor. The other Melvin Purvis." Dash slid

his fingers through Tommy's hair. "He got a call from one of my less than pleased clients about canceling the cremations. It's fine."

"Didn't sound fine." Tommy pressed kisses around the base of Dash's cock. "Sounded really not fine, to be honest."

"Well, it's not, but there's nothing I can do about it now." Dash sighed, watching Tommy's tongue slide back up his cock. "Not until we get this finished."

"What? The stuff with the Don or this blowjob?"

"Both." Dash groaned. "Come on. Just, mmm... come on, keep sucking me. Please?"

"Only because you asked so nicely." Tommy chuckled, eagerly sucking Dash into his mouth and then bobbing his head faster and harder. He swirled his tongue all around Dash's shaft, creating fantastic suction that made Dash's thighs twitch. He didn't stop or slow down until Dash was coming down his throat, and Dash melted happily into the mattress.

"I've come more today than I have in weeks," Dash mumbled drowsily.

"That's the saddest story I've ever heard." Tommy licked at Dash's cock as if he was getting ready to suck him again.

"Hey, hey!" Dash was too sensitive, and he put the heel of his hand on Tommy's forehead to push him off. "You leave that alone now. It's done. Don't even look at it."

Tommy laughed, and he crawled up to claim a kiss. "Fine, fine."

Dash enjoyed the warmth from his climax and the

sweet slide of Tommy's lips, and he scratched Tommy's scalp. "Mm, I suppose you want me to return the favor, don't you?"

"That would be very nice of you, yes." Tommy grinned. "You could even do it while I order dinner if you want."

"Or I could just do it right now."

"Now is good too."

Dash rolled Tommy over onto his back, not surprised to find him rock hard and raring to go. He took his time since this was the first blowjob he'd ever given to anyone with a dick ring, and he found that Tommy absolutely went wild when he licked around the piercing while sucking him. He wasn't a big fan of the jewelry clicking against his teeth, so he tried to keep Tommy's dick deep in the back of his throat while he sucked him.

Tommy showered him with a litany of dirty praise, and he said something in Italian when he came that sounded beautiful—but, most likely, was also very filthy.

Dash swallowed Tommy's load with a smug smile, happy that he had pleased Tommy and so quickly. He lay down beside him, a little out of breath as he said, "So. Happy now?"

"Ecstatic," Tommy replied. "Nobody's ever cleaned my pipes like that."

"Is that another maid joke?"

"I dunno. What will piss you off less?" Tommy grinned.

"How about we just order dinner and get ready for bed, huh?" Dash snorted dryly. "We have a really big day tomorrow. Making sure people stop shooting at us, clearing your name..."

"Revenge for my dad." Tommy's smile dipped.

"It's gonna be okay." Dash reached for Tommy's hand. "We got this, right? We got all that proof, we're gonna see the Don, and have lots of sex."

"You're startin' to sound like me."

"Well, I'm trying to be positive." Dash took a deep breath. "I was thinking about something Mel said. That you have to be alive to be happy. If this is the path that keeps us both alive, then yeah, I'll be happy."

"That's it? Just being alive?"

"That's not enough?"

"How about being alive, us fucking on the regular, and I get to kill the fuckin' son of bitch who killed my dad?"

"Add in getting back those funeral homes I lost as clients and I think that would be about perfect."

"Yeah, it would be. Oh! Wait." Tommy grinned. "One last thing."

"What?"

"Thinkin' about makin' my dad's ashes into a bird bath. He always liked watchin' birds and shit. Thought he'd kinda dig that."

"I think that's a great idea."

"Wait, wait! Okay, last and final thing."

Dash laughed. "What is it now?"

Tommy grabbed the remote and then slid his hand up to his hairline, wiggling his fingers around.

"Hair Waggle Guy?"

"Hair Waggle Guy."

CHAPTER 8

DASH FELL asleep in Tommy's arms, lulled to dreamland by Giorgio Tsoukalos's soothing narrative of ancient aliens in Egypt. He woke up early and then headed to the shower. Tommy stumbled into the stall with him a few minutes later. They embraced, trading kisses and hands on one another's bodies. It was slow, a yawning stretch of caresses, as neither was fully awake yet. Completion didn't feel like the goal as much as seeking out intimacy to soothe the building tension for what lay before them.

Would the proof be enough?

What if the Don simply decided to whack them both on the spot?

Tommy came first, mouthing a moan along Dash's throat. He directed his full attention to getting Dash off, and Dash let the pleasure build until he climaxed with a short shout. They held each other, and Dash was surprised and touched by the sudden tenderness. He rested his head on Tommy's shoulder, drinking in the gentle massage of Tommy's strong hands on his back, and...

"Wanna go again?" Tommy asked cheekily. "Soap is crap lube, but I can probably get a finger or two in."

So much for that.

Dash snorted and left the shower so he could get dried off and ready. He hated that they'd both be seeing the Don in clothes they'd slept in. In hindsight, they could have hung their clothing in the bathroom to soak up some of the steam, but Tommy insisted that it would be all right. The Don would understand if their shirts were a bit wrinkled.

There were far more important matters to attend to, after all.

They drove to the Don's home, the briefcase of proof sitting in Tommy's lap. The Don owned several acres north of the city, and there was a tall iron fence with a big gate discouraging wanton visitors. Dash pushed the buzzer on the intercom to announce their arrival, and the gate squealed loudly as it opened.

The drive to the house was a sprawling zigzag through trees and past a field of horses, and the house itself was a surprisingly modest ranch style home. It had a stone and brick exterior, and the front porch was framed by iron grating not too unlike the fencing that surrounded the property. The four-car garage certainly boasted of the man's wealth, as did the cars viewable within the open bay doors.

Dash didn't know much about cars, but he knew Ferraris weren't cheap.

He parked in front of the garage close to the house and took a deep breath.

Tommy reached for his hand. "Hey, don't worry. We got this."

Dash forced a smile. "Yeah."

He didn't have this. He didn't have shit except for an upset stomach and a headache. He put on his most confident facade and followed Tommy to the front door. Tommy knocked and while they were waiting for the door to open, he leaned over to kiss Dash's cheek.

"We got this," he said again.

"Yeah," Dash repeated, his heart skipping a beat. "Maybe we do."

Tommy winked.

The door opened, and it was a man with glasses flanked by two huge men in suits on the other side.

"Hagen!" Tommy greeted the bespectacled man. "Good morning."

Hagen was a small man with big eyes made more owlish by his large glasses. He was dressed in a flawless gray suit, and his gaze was sharp, scanning over Tommy and Dash as if they were specimens in a jar.

"Good morning," Dash said.

"Please. Come in." Hagen waved them both inside. As soon as the door was closed behind them, he directed the large men, "Search them."

Dash and Tommy raised their hands, consenting to the pat down. Tommy had to give up his guns, plus two knives and a pair of brass knuckles Dash hadn't even seen. Dash had nothing except his phones, but those were taken too.

"You'll get everything back when our business is concluded," Hagen explained. "Can't be too careful these days."

"No shit," Tommy grumbled.

"The briefcase?" Hagen nodded at it. "Please open it."

Tommy did as he was asked, showing Hagen there was nothing inside but folders and papers.

Hagen seemed to relax, and he even smiled now. "Thank you. Now. Are you hungry? Have you had breakfast yet?"

"No. Kinda rushed to get over here." Tommy frowned. "Where is the Don?"

"He's resting. His last treatment was hard on him."

"Treatment for fuckin' what?"

"I'll explain everything," Hagen promised. "Now please. What would you like for breakfast? Our chef is at your disposal."

"Uh, egg whites and toast with some strawberry preserves." Tommy patted his stomach. "Just to be safe."

"Still having gallbladder trouble, eh?" Hagen chuckled. "My wife's was much the same when she had hers taken out."

"Fuckin' sucks."

"And you, sir?" Hagen asked Dash. "I'm sorry that we haven't had the pleasure." He held out his hand.

"Jonah," Dash replied quickly. He didn't know why, but he didn't want to give his Purvis name. "I'm a friend of Tommy's."

"Ah, so. And what would you like to eat?"

"Sausage biscuit? Maybe some gravy?"

"Absolutely." Hagen nodded to the one of the large

suited men. "Pass that along to the chef. Now, you two." He waved at Dash and Tommy. "Come, come." He led them through the home toward a set of French doors that opened up to a large screened-in back porch.

Dash managed a quick glance around, finding the interior of the house quietly decorated in tans and beiges. It looked like a house that had been staged by a realtor and didn't show any signs of being truly lived in or any personal touches except for the collages of framed photos. A few were black and white, showing who Dash assumed was the Don and his wife.

There was another photo right next to it with a different woman, so...

Girlfriend? Maybe?

He didn't have long to think about it, now taking his seat beside Tommy at a glass-top patio table. The furniture was plush, expensive, and Dash drooled when he saw a fresh pot of coffee waiting for them.

"Coffee? Water?" Hagen offered.

"Coffee, yes. Thank you." Dash reached for the pot and grabbed a cup to serve himself.

That's when he noticed there was an honest to God butler waiting to pour, and he relented his grip on the coffee pot. The butler smiled politely and finished pouring.

"Sugar? Creamer?" the butler asked.

"No, thank you." Dash decided today was a black coffee sort of morning and took a cautious sip.

"Same for me," Tommy said. "Thanks."

The butler poured another mug for Tommy, and then he looked to Hagen.

"I'm fine, thank you." Hagen nodded. "Please let the chef know we're ready to eat."

"Right away, sir." The butler headed back inside the house.

The large men were hovering by the door, but they didn't come outside.

Once the door shut, Hagen spoke. "Now. This stays here and does not leave this table. Do you both understand?"

"Yeah, of course." Tommy frowned and leaned forward in his chair. "What's going on?"

"The Don is sick," Hagen replied. "Kidney failure. He's having dialysis done three times a week now. We're having the arrangements made so he can have the treatments here at home instead of having to travel to the clinic. Hopefully by next week."

"Fuck. How... How bad is it?"

"Bad," Hagen replied curtly. "I suspect it has been the catalyst for this recent... unpleasantness."

Tommy narrowed his eyes. "You think Dio took out my dad 'cause he's lookin' to be the next fuckin' Don?"

Hagen sighed. "It's nothing I can say for certain, but I do find it rather convenient that he's decided to start a war in the family right when our Don has fallen ill. He's painting himself as the hero cleansing the corruption from our ranks, but if what you say is true, he's actually the rot that we need to prune."

"It is." Tommy put the briefcase on the table. "Inside are bank statements from a dummy fuckin' account. Look at the page with the highlights right on top."

Hagen popped open the briefcase. "And what is it

you think I'm looking at?" He picked up the page, squinting at it.

"We never write checks out for fuckin' nothin'," Tommy replied urgently. "Look at the amounts. Dio was funneling money through this account and scrapin' some for himself right off the top. I'd need our books to confirm it, but I am fuckin' positive this is the money we've been losing."

Hagen reached for the other papers. He was quiet as he read over them, his lips moving silently here and there.

Tommy fidgeted, and he added, "I'm sure it would add up to the same amount we're missing, you know. I dunno who that is on the account, but I bet it's one of my uncle's fake names or somethin'. I, uh, I also confirmed that number written up there? That's one of our family accounts, and it's the same one that paid the cleaner."

"Really?" That drew Hagen's attention, and he frowned at Tommy.

"Yup. And it was definitely my uncle's men who came after me at my apartment, yeah?"

"Yes." Hagen nodded. "The ones you killed at your apartment were. He also said there are two more missing as well. I don't suppose you know anything about that?"

"Were they at my dad's place?"

"Yes."

"Yeah, well, I can tell you he ain't gonna find 'em. They tried to fuckin' kill me too."

"Your uncle sincerely believes you are the thief."

"I can sincerely tell you that I'm not!" Tommy gestured to the briefcase. "My dad had me wearin' a fuckin' wire workin' with Detective Darcey tryin' to catch him! Come on. Look at all this."

"This could also easily be construed as evidence that you are, in fact, a police informant."

"Yeah, but..." Tommy scoffed. "I'm *not*."

Hagen closed the briefcase. "I am going to take this to the Don right now."

Tommy stood up from his seat. "Okay, finally! Let's go."

"No." Hagen gestured for Tommy to sit back down. "Stay here. Enjoy your breakfast. I promise you'll be able to see him before he makes a decision, all right?"

Tommy narrowed his eyes, and he visibly tensed. "Come on, Hagen. He's my grandpa too, you know. I wanna fuckin' see him right now."

"And your grandfather is very sick. Please give me just a few minutes to speak with him."

Dash froze, unsure as to what Tommy was going to do next. He looked ready to jump across the table and punch Hagen right in the mouth. Dash wagered he might be able to get through the screen and run around to grab the car before those big guys who were certainly armed came to get them.

Maybe.

"Hey." Hagen offered a sympathetic smile. "You'll be able to see him soon."

The tension ebbed, and Tommy slowly took his seat again. "Okay, fine. Just, you know... tell him I said hi and shit, all right?"

"Of course."

Dash slurped his coffee.

"I'll be right back. The chef should be out with your food soon." Hagen took the briefcase and then stepped back inside the house.

Dash let out a breath he hadn't realized he'd been holding. "Well, shit. I think that went... well?"

"I guess." Tommy frowned.

"What's wrong?"

"I can't believe my grandpa is so fuckin' sick. Nobody told me."

"It sounds like they've been keeping it a secret." Dash took another sip of coffee. "In my experience, it's not abnormal for families to lie about that stuff. They don't want anyone to worry about them."

"Or think they look weak," Tommy added thoughtfully. "Maybe this is why Dio decided to start shit now. With my dad dead, my uncle would be the next in line to take over the family if my grandpa dies."

"Would explain too why he's so desperate to kill you. Pretty sure the rest of the family isn't gonna be too happy with him if they find out he killed your dad and tried to kill you."

"Nope."

The door opened, and an older man with bushy eyebrows came out carrying a tray of food. He had a friendly smile, and he asked, "Who had the egg whites?"

"Me." Tommy raised his hand.

"Here you go, sir." The chef set down the plate and silverware, and then turned to Dash. "The sausage biscuit and gravy?"

"Yes, sir. Thank you," Dash said.

The chef put the other plate and another set of silverware in front of Dash. "There we are. Can I get you gentlemen anything else?"

"No, thanks." Tommy looked to Dash.

Dash shook his head. He couldn't speak because he'd already shoved a giant forkful in his mouth. He thought he heard someone yelling inside the house, but he couldn't be sure.

"Enjoy, gentlemen." The chef bowed before heading back to the door. When he opened it, a man was clearly shouting.

"I wanna know where the fuck he is right fuckin' now!" the man raged.

"For fuck's sake! Dio!" Hagen snapped. "Stop this now!"

"Not until you tell me where that lil' shit is!"

Tommy and Dash both froze, and the door shut, muffling the argument.

They knew that voice.

"That's my fuckin' uncle." Tommy jumped to his feet. "Fuck!"

"What do we do?" Dash asked through a bite of biscuit. "Do we run?"

"Fuck yes, we run!" Tommy grabbed a butter knife from the table and then bolted to the screen door. "Those fuckers took my guns and my uncle sounds fuckin' pissed."

"I still got my keys." Dash followed behind Tommy.

"Good." Tommy hurried through the door, reaching back for Dash's hand. "We're gonna haul ass the fuck out of here. This is bullshit."

"Do you think Hagen set us up?"

"I dunno." Tommy ran around the corner of the house, nearly smacking into the air conditioning unit. He paused at the next turn, peeking around to the front yard. "Shit."

"What?"

"More of my uncle's fuckin' guys. Standin' right there by your car."

"Shit." Dash gritted his teeth. "Now what?"

"Fuck. Hang on, I'm thinkin'." Tommy nudged Dash back toward the air conditioning unit near the back corner of the house. "We can't make it to your car without gettin' popped and we sure as shit can't stay on that porch like sittin' fuckin' ducks either. We might be able to sneak into the garage if we go around the other side of the house, but then we're cornered unless you know how to hotwire a Ferrari in ten seconds."

Dash looked around. "Can we just run for it?"

"What? Off into the trees? Go hide behind a horse?"

"I don't know! I'm just trying to think!"

"I know! I'm sorry, okay? We just need to—"

The back doors flew open, Dio's voice loud and clear as he shouted, "You are so full of shit! Where the fuck is my nephew, huh?"

"I have no idea," Hagen retorted coolly. "Now if you'll excuse me, I was in the middle of my breakfast."

Dash and Tommy exchanged a quick glance. It sounded like Hagen was covering for them. Even so, Dash was already eyeing the trees and wondering how fast he could run with all the adrenaline racing through his body right now.

"Yeah, I'm real fuckin' sure," Dio sneered. "You listen

to me, you lil' fuck. I'm going to get my nephew and if I find out you were involved with any of this shit, you're fucking dead."

"A pleasure as always, Dio."

"Fuck off." The door opened and then slammed shut.

Dash and Tommy flinched, and Dash squeezed Tommy's hand.

Tommy still had the butter knife, and Dash had no doubt that Tommy could take down at least one or two of Dio's men with that thing. It still wasn't very comforting since Dash would probably be dead by that point, but he hoped he'd get to see Tommy be a badass one last time.

The seconds ticked by slowly, filled only by an agonizing silence that seemed to stretch on for an eternity. Dash's pulse was pounding in his ears, and he could feel it throbbing where he was holding Tommy's hand so tightly.

Tommy looked at Dash over his shoulder, and he smiled, bright and confident as ever.

Dash wished he felt half as sure as he did, but he tried to smile back.

He really, really wanted to make it out of this shit alive with Tommy and order more greasy pizza and cuddle on the couch and maybe try sex with the dick ring in—

A car door opened and shut. Then another. And another.

Tommy's smile vanished as he listened.

"Are they going?" Dash whispered.

The car started.

"Either way, we gotta move," Tommy whispered back. "As soon as they pull down the drive, they're gonna see us standing here."

"What if we duck behind the AC unit?"

"We are not both gonna fit there."

"We could try!"

"Gentlemen?" Hagen called out, his voice soft but urgent. "Where are you?"

Tommy poked his head back around the corner to peek at the porch. He looked back at Dash and nodded. "It's just Hagen." He went first with Dash following behind and stepped back onto the porch. "Well, that was fuckin' fun. *Not.*"

"My apologies." Hagen appeared distressed. "I expected that Dio might show up at some point, but I didn't expect him to be so brash."

"Can I go see the Don yet?" Tommy demanded.

"There's no need. Please. Sit down." Hagen gestured to the table. "I have good news."

"I'm not sittin' until I know whether or not I gotta run."

"I assume it's all right to talk in front of your... friend?" Hagen frowned at Dash.

"He's my family," Tommy said without hesitation. "Could take the wings off a fly at a hundred yards, no problem. So, you tell me, are we stayin' or are we runnin'?"

Dash did his best to look intimidating. He didn't think it was working.

"Very well," Hagen said. "The Don has declared Dio a traitor and wants him removed by you personally."

Tommy blinked. "No shit?"

Dash sighed in relief and immediately flopped into his chair.

"Yes," Hagen confirmed. "He found the evidence you presented most compelling, and the family cannot afford to lose another dime. We have no idea how much your uncle pissed away, not to mention he blew over a hundred thousand dollars on the cleaner and then expected me to compensate him for it!"

Dash choked on air.

"Over a hundred grand, huh?" Tommy echoed.

"Well, it *was* supposed to be a hundred and twenty-five." Hagen chuckled. "Dio should ask for a refund seeing as how you're alive, but I don't think he's going to have the chance to."

"Damn right." Tommy grinned. "We're gonna get the son of a bitch. As soon as we leave here, I'll see who I can round up and we'll hit him hard." He took a big bite of eggs, smearing some preserves over his top lip.

Dash urgently tapped Tommy's leg.

"What?" Tommy blinked.

Dash tried to use his eyes and glance toward the house as subtly as he could.

"What is it?" Tommy frowned, clearly not under-standing.

"Oh, you've got a little something." Hagen gestured to his face. "Some jelly."

"Huh?" Tommy touched his mouth. When he found the preserves, he laughed. "Oh, makin' a mess, huh?"

"Trying to look like your father now?" Hagen teased.

Tommy picked up a napkin and wiped off his mouth,

chuckling. "Just keeping his memory alive. I don't think I could rock the 'stache like he could though."

Oh, for the love of God.

Dash wanted to *scream*.

"May I use your bathroom?" Dash said quickly.

Hagen nodded. "Of course. First door on your left down the hall."

Dash reached for Tommy's leg under the table. "Can you come show me?"

"What? Right now?" Tommy scoffed. "Kinda in the middle of talkin' some business."

"Yes. And that's... gotten me... so hot." Dash couldn't believe what he was saying. "This might be the last time I see you. Uh, this is so dangerous. And sexy. And I really, really need to be alone with you. Right now."

Tommy grinned, but then he cleared his throat, glancing at Hagen. "You, uh, you okay with giving us a few minutes?"

"I heard absolutely nothing." Hagen glanced at the ceiling with a haggard sigh. "Try not to... take too long doing whatever it is you're doing."

"Cool. Thanks, Hagen." Tommy stood from the table, leading the way inside with a strut in his step.

Dash followed close behind, and he tried to do his best to look like someone who really wanted to fuck and not someone who was absolutely terrified. He glanced warily at the armed men by the door, wishing there was another way out of this house.

Maybe there would be a window. He and Tommy could go out through the window, get to the car, drive away, and just leave town. They could go see Mel in Florida; that would be great and they'd both be alive.

Tommy opened the bathroom door, ushering Dash inside.

Dash grimaced when he saw that there was a window, but there was no way he or Tommy would ever fit through.

So much for that plan.

Tommy shut the door behind them, saying, "Okay, as much as I want to make a million fuckin' jokes about getting you to go to the bathroom with me, what the fuck?"

"We have to leave right now," Dash said quickly.

"Why?"

"It's Hagen! It's him—"

"*What?*"

"Listen to me." Dash took a deep breath. "It's twenty-five grand to clean a problem. He just said the cleaner was supposed to cost a hundred and twenty-five grand, right? And that Dio needed to get a refund because you're alive?"

"I'm so bad at math. Explain please."

"It's only over a hundred grand with *five* bodies. You never told Hagen how your father died, just that he was dead and your uncle killed him. Only one person would know your father was at that fucking house."

"One person..." Tommy's eyes widened. "The person who killed him."

"Which can't be Dio. Dio is after you for killing your father, right?"

"And being a snitch and some other dumb shit."

"Okay, and we know that's impossible since your father was dead in the same house as you. There's no way you could have done it, and I was paid for *four*. The only person who could know there was a fifth body there would be the guy who helped put him there."

"Son of a bitch."

"And then that comment about the mustache! Didn't you tell me your dad had just shaved his beard?"

"Yeah?" Tommy frowned.

"Hagen said your father hadn't been by here in a week or two. How did he know he had a mustache now? He knows because he fuckin' saw it when he killed him at Darcey's place!"

"Son of a *bitch*."

The bathroom door suddenly busted open, pieces of the frame splintering.

"Thank you," Hagen said politely to the large man who had just kicked it open. He smiled at Tommy and Dash. "Let's try this again, shall we?"

"*You* motherfucker." Tommy's eyes narrowed, and he stood in front of Dash.

"Yes, yes, me." Hagen raised a gun, aiming it at Tommy, but he was looking at Dash over his shoulder. "Jonah, I believe you said? Also known as Melvin Purvis, I assume?"

Dash put his hand on Tommy's shoulder. "The one and only."

"Sorry that I didn't recognize you. I thought you were one of Tommaso's passing amusements. That bit about the wings off a fly was a nice touch, but as usual,

Tommaso is full of shit." He scoffed. "You two have been making an awful lot of trouble for me."

"That account is yours, isn't it?" Tommy demanded. "You're the one who's been stealing money from the fuckin' family!"

"Let's not do this whole villainous exposition thing, all right? It's a little cliché." Hagen sighed. "It's much easier if you just go ahead and die. You can do that, can't you? Might be the first thing in your whole life that you don't fuck up."

"Fuck you—"

The gun fired.

Tommy flinched, Dash closed his eyes, and then...

More shots went off, two to be exact.

Tommy was still standing, and Dash had to open his eyes.

Hagen was on the floor, dead. The two large men were crumpled in the hallway behind him, equally lifeless. Someone was coming in now, stepping over the bodies with a nasty scowl, and Dash didn't know whether he should throw up or laugh or cry.

It was Dio Capelli.

CHAPTER 9

"DIO?" Tommy spat, confused and angry. "What the fuck?"

"How about a lil' fuckin' gratitude, you lil' shit?" Dio barked back. "Come on now, I just saved your fuckin' life!" He eyed Dash. "You too, Mr. Purvis!"

"What the fuck is going on?" Dash demanded furiously.

He'd been seconds away from possibly dying—*again*—and he'd officially reached his breaking point. He didn't care that he needed to be thankful. After everything that had happened, he was pissed off.

"What's goin' on is I'm not as stupid as that lil' snobby shit thinks I am," Dio replied with a smug smirk. He holstered his gun. "Let's fuckin' go, huh? I need a fuckin' drink."

Tommy blinked slowly. "Okay, wait. I am very confused. I thought you wanted me dead."

"I did. Now I don't." Dio nodded his head toward the hall. "Let's go already."

Tommy hesitated, but then he followed after Dio, being mindful of the blood.

Dash tiptoed with equal care, and he trailed behind as they all went into the living room. He was startled to see eight suited men clustered around the door, and they were definitely armed to the teeth.

"Go on." Dio waved at the men. "Check the rest of the house just in case. See if that worm had anybody else hidin' out here." He pointed at one guy. "Except you. You, go get me a fuckin' drink. Just bring the bottle." He sat down heavily in a chair, and he gestured for Tommy and Dash to sit on the couch across from him. "Let's talk, huh?"

Tommy sat first, waiting for Dash to join him before he snapped, "What in the actual fuck is going on, huh? Hagen had it comin' and all, but—"

"Because, you dumb lil' shit, I'm good at my fuckin' job!" Dio rolled his eyes. "Yeah, I thought it was you that was stealin' from us and talkin' to the cops. I knew you had a wire on that night in the club, and so I called Hagen, told him what was up. He said the Don wanted me to handle you personally."

"Yeah, sure he did." Tommy scowled. "Why don't we go talk to the Don, huh? See what he has to say?"

"Nothin'."

"What?"

"He's gonna say a whole lot of fuckin' nothin'." Dio grew somber. "He can't say nothin' at all now 'cause he's dead."

"What?" Tommy's eyes widened.

"Funny thing. Some funeral home called me last

night to let me know that his cremation had been rescheduled and to apologize for the *repeated* delay in getting his ashes back to me. I said, *what fuckin' cremation?*" Dio grimaced. "I demanded to see the body, and they ran over to the crematory to get him for me first thing this morning. The place won't open, so I got my men to help them get in. It's him."

Tommy tensed.

Dash cleared his throat. "What, uh, crematory was this?"

"Yours," Dio replied bluntly.

"We were just there! You're tellin' me I was literally hanging out in the same building as my dead fuckin' grandpa?" Tommy frowned at Dash. "You didn't think to mention you had some other Capelli fellow layin' around?"

"There aren't any!" Dash scowled. "I would have remembered that!"

"The Don went back to using the family name a few years ago, *Capellinio,*" Dio explained. "Not the bullshit *Capelli* we all got smacked with at Ellis Island, all right?"

"Shit. Yes. Capellinio. He had a preneed, didn't he?" Dash asked.

"And how the fuck do you know that? They send it to you or somethin'?"

"No, the funeral home called me about him. The director working with the family was mad because I didn't have the urn listed on the preneed and the cremation got rescheduled a few times in light of the, uh, current situation. After I had to cancel it, he must have called the phone number on the file and not whatever number Hagen gave them."

"Yeah, fuckers called the damn landline at my house." Dio laughed. "Imagine that, huh?"

"You still have a landline?" Tommy asked.

"Shut up. It's a good thing I still do or I wouldn't have found out the Don was dead."

"Okay, fair."

The man Dio had instructed to find alcohol returned with a bottle and three glasses. He set the glasses down first and then started to pour.

"Hey, hey, I can still pour my own booze. Go on. Go watch the wall or somethin'." Dio shooed him away and grabbed the bottle to fill his glass. He left the other two glasses for Tommy and Dash to pour themselves.

Tommy only gave Dash a splash, but he filled his glass as high as his uncle had.

"Anyway." Dio took a big gulp. "So, here I was knowin' the Don is dead and that Hagen is full of shit. I think maybe that you're in it with him, but then word gets out that Detective Darcey, Leo's grade school buddy, happens to be missin'. My guys confirm he's the cop they blew away, and I realize Darcey must be the one who wired you up.

"Your old man did always love him some sneaky shit, and it wouldn't be the first time he's done some crap like this. Leo's the one who vouched for you to come work with me, you know. I think some more about it. I know I'm not stealin', and it doesn't really make any sense for you to be the one stealin'—"

"Aw, thanks." Tommy grinned. "I appreciate that, Uncle."

"Yeah, because you're an idiot." Dio snorted. "Come on, kid. I figured out you were wearin' a fuckin' wire because you wouldn't stop scratching at it."

"It itched. They told me to shave."

"After havin' my little think, I realized Hagen was setting us both up real pretty. He wasn't gonna stop until I killed you just to get you out of his way."

"He wanted me to kill you too."

"It's cute that you woulda tried." Dio smirked. "Good thing I was waitin' just down the road for ya', huh? Now we're both nice and alive."

"Yeah." Tommy paused for a moment. "And you were waiting why exactly? How did you know I was here?"

"The food. On the porch."

"What?"

"The egg whites and strawberry jelly, hello. Who the fuck else eats that nasty shit? Plus, Mr. Purvis's car bein' here was a pretty big damn clue." He eyed Dash. "I looked you up once Hagen told me Tommaso was still alive. Was a bit sore you took my hundred grand if you only cleaned up three bodies."

"Technically, I still cleaned four," Dash said.

"Four?"

"Dad," Tommy added quietly. "He was at the house."

Dio said something in Italian, probably a curse. "So, Leo *is* dead. Was hoping that was more of Hagen's bull-shit and maybe he was just hidin' out somewhere."

"I found him at the house you sent me to clean,"

Dash explained. "I didn't know who he was until I saw a picture of him later and Tommy told me."

"What the fuck was he doing there?" Dio demanded.

"I think Darcey called him," Tommy replied. "We found this note with all the evidence Darcey stashed. He left it all in this hiding spot they used as kids for him to find. I'm pretty sure Darcey knew we were going down and my dad wouldn't be there until it was too late."

"Yeah." Dio made a face. "Too late is right. My guys would have said somethin' if they'd seen Leo there, and nobody saw nothin'."

"It must have been Hagen or one of his guys, right?"

"Yeah. Leo probably called Hagen to tell him what the fuck was going on. Somethin' this big, he would have wanted the Don involved. I bet Hagen hauled ass over there to wait for Leo. Maybe he was lookin' for the evidence too, if Leo even mentioned all that, but I bet he couldn't pass up a chance to kill your old man."

"But why?" Dash blurted out. "Why was Hagen killing off the Capelli family? He worked for you."

"Yeah, *worked* for us, but he's not *one* of us," Dio replied. "He was lucky to have the position that he did, that fucker. He probably figured he could keep sending out orders after the Don was dead and keep bullshitting us for a while. But he knew that wouldn't last forever, so he had to figure out how to get rid of anybody who was in line to take the reins. Me, Tommy, and his father. He sets me up to knock off Tommy and then Leo calls him, so he jumps on his chance to take him out over at Darcey's. When he found out Tommy was still alive, he decided to play the two of us against each other."

"How did you find out I was alive anyway?" Tommy asked.

"You dumbass. Hagen *told* me."

"Oh. Well, fuck." Tommy slouched back against the cushions. "That fuckin' prick."

"I figured it was only a matter of time before Hagen sent you after me or, the much more likely option, decided to quit playin' around and tried to kill you himself." Dio took a long sip of his drink. "I knew you were still alive at least once I saw the plates, so I backed off, waited a bit, and then I told my men that we were goin' in guns fuckin' blazing."

"For which, I am very thankful."

"Ditto," Dash added.

"What happens now?" Tommy asked, frowning a bit. "I guess we're talkin' with the new Don, right? Seein' as how there ain't nobody else left."

"We'll worry about that shit later," Dio replied. "We gotta make sure there's nobody else left who was loyal to Hagen and tighten up the fuckin' ranks. We get whatever's left of the money that piece of shit took from us and we move on. We got some fuckin' funerals to attend, all right? It ain't gonna be fun."

"What about, uh, the little mess at my apartment?"

"*Little mess?*"

"You know, the mess at my apartment?"

"Yeah, come here. Come here for just a second." Dio beckoned Tommy closer with a finger. "Just come over here."

Tommy stood, slowly leaning over toward Dio.

Dio waited until Tommy was close enough and then

he smacked the side of his head. "Little fuckin' mess, my ass! That's for killin' my guys, you little shit."

"Ow! Hey!" Tommy scowled and rubbed his head as he sat back down. He grabbed his glass. "Would you be happier if they had killed me?"

"Fuckin' maybe."

Tommy snorted and then gulped back his booze.

Dio scoffed. "Now listen, we gotta sell it as a break-in and you were acting in self-defense, all right? That's the only way we get through it 'cause the cops are already sniffin' our butts."

"What about the guys you had up at my dad's place?"

"They ran away together, I don't fuckin' know!" Dio drank more. "One fuckin' headache at a time." He looked at Dash. "I'm assumin' you helped with that, Mr. Purvis?"

"I did," Dash replied.

"Good." Dio smirked. "You can go help with the problems in the bathroom."

"That'll be seventy-five thousand dollars, Mr. Capelli."

"Uh, it'll be seventy-five fuckin' nothin'. Consider it your apology to me since you didn't call me when you found my nephew alive."

Dash cringed. "Of course, sir."

Tommy slapped a hand on Dash's thigh as he turned his drink up. "Rough luck, maid."

"Shut it, accountant."

Tommy cackled under his breath, pouring them both another drink. He offered some more to Dio, and Dio waved him on so he filled his glass again. "So, uh. What are we doing with Grandpa then?"

"We get his ass cremated and then he's goin' to Italy to Brolio Castle. Oldest winery in the whole country, Barone Ricasoli, is over there, and he wanted to be spread right out in front so he could look at it or somethin'." Dio paused. "Where is your father?"

"Cremated in a bag of Kwik-Krete." Tommy forced a smile. "Thought maybe they could go together."

"Fuck it." Dio sighed. "I'll see if I can get the priest to do last rites."

"For a bag of concrete?"

"He'll do whatever the fuck I pay him to do." Dio scowled heavily. "Ain't Leo's fault he got murdered." He sat back, massaging his forehead. "Mr. Purvis, what do you need to clean?"

"I need to go get my van." Dash hesitated. "I'm guessing you guys broke into my place?"

"You would guess correctly, sir."

Dash knew that meant it was completely trashed. "I can be back in about an hour."

Dio waved at Tommy. "Go with him. Get whatever he needs."

"Really?" Tommy seemed surprised.

"You was already gonna ask me to go, so just fuckin' go."

"How did—"

"*Not stupid.*" Dio waved again, this time at his men. "Help 'em find their weapons, phones, whatever else shit they got here. We're gettin' the fuck out."

"Where are you going?" Tommy asked.

"I'm going back to the house to start my own kinda cleaning," Dio replied. "Let the rest of the family know what the fuck happened and what we're gonna do to save some face. Don't look good, one of our own got the best of us. We can't look weak and we gotta get back in control fast. Don't you worry." He smirked. "I got this."

Tommy polished off his drink. "All right, Uncle."

Dash hadn't touched his glass, and he tried not to laugh when Tommy grabbed it to finish it for him. He offered his hand to Dio, saying, "Thank you, sir. I promise I'll take care of this with the utmost professional—"

"Mr. Purvis?" Dio shook Dash's hand. "Please just get the fuckin' corpses out, okay?"

"Yes, sir."

Tommy stood, but then he kneeled before Dio. They both looked at each other for a long moment, wordlessly taking in the many emotions certainly warring between them. Dio had tried to kill him, Tommy had certainly agreed to try and kill him right back, but in this moment...

They were two men who had lost a lot of family and friends over the last few days.

Dio patted Tommy's shoulder and gave him a sad smile.

Tommy's eyes got damp, and he took Dio's hand. Then he leaned in as if he was about to kiss it.

"Easy, easy!" Dio swatted him away, breaking the tension. "I'm not the fuckin' Don yet. Save those pretty lips for your damn maid. Now go on."

"Right." Tommy quickly stood up, sniffing and playing off the emotional moment. "We're goin'."

Once Dash had his phones back and Tommy his weapons, they left the house and then sat in the car. Dash had cranked the engine, but he needed a moment before they went anywhere.

He leaned over the seat and dragged Tommy into a deep kiss.

"Mmm, *baby*." Tommy grinned hungrily. "I need to get some more of that pronto."

"Once we are far, far away from the latest place we've almost died," Dash promised, taking Tommy's hand.

"You fuckin' got it." Tommy kissed Dash again, and it was sweeter and slower than before. "Mm, just one more."

"Just one," Dash mumbled, though it was hard to talk over Tommy's tongue. He knew they needed to go, but he was jittery and had nowhere to put all of this nervous energy. Kissing Tommy felt so good and right, and he—

His phone rang.

"Shit." Dash fumbled around in his pocket.

"To be continued," Tommy said, running his tongue over his lips.

"To be continued," Dash agreed as he finally freed his phone and saw who it was just as the call went to voicemail. "Shit."

"Who is it?"

"It's Mel." Dash grimaced. "He's called eleven times. Shit, shit, shit." He quickly called him back.

"Aw, he was worried," Tommy cooed. "How sweet."

"This had better be you and you'd better be dead 'cause if you were alive all this damn time and didn't fuckin' answer me, you're gonna wish you were dead!" Mel shouted through the line.

"Hey, hey! It's me!" Dash cringed. "I'm sorry, we're okay. We're both okay."

"I don't give a fuck about that other idiot!"

Tommy pouted dramatically.

"I've been worried half to damn death," Mel raged on. "I thought I was gonna have to fly my old ass up there and take on the whole Capelli family all by myself!"

"No, hey, it's all right," Dash insisted. "We got it all taken care of, okay?"

"What the fuck happened? Your proof worked out then, huh?"

"Kinda." Dash made a face. "Turns out Hagen is the one who was stealing money from the family and was hiding the Don's death from everyone."

"Olimpio is dead too? *Christ.*"

"Natural causes. I think. Anyway. Hagen was acting like he was still alive and ordering everybody around, trying to get the family to bump each other off. It almost worked too, but Tommy's uncle got wise and saved the day."

"And you too!" Tommy piped up. "You did the thing with the four and the five! And the jelly!"

"What's he saying now?" Mel asked.

"Nothing. I, uh, maybe figured out Hagen was lying about some stuff. No big deal."

"Hey, whatever you did, I'm glad you finally made

time on your busy schedule to call back an old man." Mel sounded like he was smiling.

"I'm glad too." Dash beamed.

"I'm assuming you've got some cleaning to do?"

"Yeah. I'll call you later tonight, all right?"

"Call me tomorrow. I'm taking a Valium and then a nap. I can't handle this kinda stress, kid." Mel snorted. "Don't forget. You still got a bunch of ass to kiss."

"On it. I haven't forgotten about the kissing of the ass."

"You take care, kid. And you tell Tommaso to act right. I can still clean."

Dash chuckled. "Will do, Mel."

"Bye now."

"Bye."

"I could only hear about every other word," Tommy said, "but I do believe that man threatened me."

"He did." Dash stuck his phone in the cup holder and then backed up, carefully navigating around the other cars that were here now.

The last thing he wanted to do was ding the new Don's ride.

"That's thoughtful of him," Tommy teased. "It's nice to know he cares, huh?"

"He's a good man." Dash chuckled. "One of a kind, that's for sure. He had all sorts of funny sayings for everything. No matter what the situation was, he had some little bit of wisdom to share."

"Yeah? Like what?"

"Like when we had to clean up the crematory floor because a container we received was leaking—"

"Wait, wait, a container? As in the thing with the body in it?"

"Yup."

"And it was leaking *what*?"

"You probably don't want to know. Anyway." Dash chuckled. "We're down on our hands and knees, scooping up all this junk, disinfecting the hell out of everything, and I'm pissed. I was tired, I didn't want to be there, I wanted to go the hell home, and Mel looks at me. He just looks at me with this big stupid grin and says *any day above ground is a good day*."

Tommy went quiet for a moment. "Any day above ground is a good day," he repeated thoughtfully. "Huh. I like that."

"Even the shit days are good days if you're around to complain about 'em, you know?"

"What the fuck would you call the days we've been havin', huh?" Tommy cackled.

Dash glanced at the horses as he drove by the field, saying, "I literally wondered if those horses would make good shields today. I would say the last forty-eight whatever hours have been a few levels above *shit*."

"You know horses aren't bulletproof, right?"

"Yes, I know—"

"The horse would have died, Dash. That's just sick."

"It was *your* idea, for the love of—"

"You're a sick, sick man." Tommy grinned.

Dash tried not to laugh, but he couldn't stop. It felt too good, eased his nervous energy, and he smiled when Tommy dropped his hand on his knee. They'd reached

ACE OF MAIDS   163

the gate now and had to wait for it to open, and Dash looked over at Tommy's ridiculous smile.

He could imagine seeing that beautiful face every single day for a very, very long time.

Dash wanted to learn how to cook for him, make messes in the kitchen together, lounge around playing video games and talking for hours on end, let Tommy pirate movies for them to watch, and...

Wow.

Dash could see a future with Tommy.

It was startling how easy it was to see himself building a life with this wild gangster he'd only spent a few days with. Granted, the days had been by far the craziest of his entire life—and that was saying a lot for someone who cleaned problems for a living. Everything was easy with Tommy, probably in part because Dash knew he didn't have anything to hide from him. He could be himself, totally and and fully transparent with everything, and he could imagine himself being with Tommy for a very long time.

Perhaps even forever.

"Hey, I do work with dead people," Dash pointed out, quickly withdrawing from his daydream to pull through the gate. "I'm pretty twisted."

"And you totally believe in aliens," Tommy teased.

"Hey!" Dash narrowed his eyes. "I said that I believe in the *possibility* of aliens."

Okay, strong maybe on the forever part.

"That's not what you said when we were watching Hair Waggle. You were all, *wow, look at that, yes,* it was aliens."

"I did not!" Dash laughed.

"So, uh, unrelated question, but since my place is literally a crime scene, don't suppose I could crash with you for a few days?"

"You just made fun of me for believing in aliens." Dash was tempted to brake check Tommy once they got back out on the main road, but he resisted. "Sounds like you better find a hotel or something."

"Are you coming with me to said hotel?"

"Maybe."

"Just sayin', your place got trashed, right? We could grab some clothes, find your maid outfit, get some food on the way..."

"And go back to the hotel, huh? Just like that?"

"That was sort of my plan." Tommy smirked. "I've gotten kinda used to having you around, you know." He squeezed Dash's knee. "Thought maybe... you'd be okay with spending a little bit more time with me."

"I might be."

"Can't say that I would have made it through this shit without you. Hell, I wouldn't be sitting here if it wasn't for you." Tommy slid his hand up to take Dash's. "You saved my life."

"You saved mine, more than once." Dash's pulse sped up, and he adjusted his glasses. "I think we're pretty even."

"Nah."

"You stabbed someone in the eye for me."

"No shit!" Tommy laughed. "Oh, I did, didn't I?"

Dash chuckled. "Yeah, you did. Might just be the most romantic thing anyone's ever done for me."

"The very fact that you find that romantic is getting me so fuckin' hard right now."

"For fuck's sake." Dash groaned. "Really? Right this very second?"

"Hard as a fuckin' rock."

"We still have to come back and clean up three bodies. You know that, right?"

"So." Tommy clicked his tongue. "A quickie?"

"Seriously?" Dash groaned again, trying not to smile. "We'll see."

Tommy grinned triumphantly.

"That was *not* a yes."

"Close enough." Tommy adjusted himself. "You're a hell of a guy, Jonah."

Dash's heart skipped over itself. "Yeah? So are you, Tommaso."

"You're a hell of a maid too."

"Shut up."

DASH STAYED busy working at the crematory and cleaning up problems for the new Don of the Capelli family. Dio was right in that there were those loyal to Hagen who had been waiting for him to make a move and take over, and Dio crushed them, cementing his place as head of the family and his legacy as a merciless leader.

Dash was glad he was on Dio's good side.

The Capelli family had services for both the recently deceased Don and Tommy's father, Leonardo. Dash didn't get into the particulars of how they managed to get Leonardo's death to not arouse suspicion or how much of the Kwik-Krete bag was actually present in the urn, but Tommy seemed glad to put it all behind him.

Dash and Tommy continued to see each other frequently, though Tommy was often tied up with family business. Dio was now grooming Tommy to take over the finance department that he once led, and Tommy said it was many long nights of counting, recounting, beating people, and then counting again.

The "little mess" at Tommy's apartment disappeared, and Dash was surprised he never had to speak to the cops. It was simply as if it had never happened, same with the men Tommy had killed over at his father's house, not to mention the others killed over at Darcey's and Darcey himself.

The family's power was startling and reminded Dash how dangerous this life was. He had spent so long merely tidying up the aftermath that he'd become a bit oblivious to the risks. His adventure with Tommy was a hell of a wake-up call, and he vowed to be even more cautious than ever. It wasn't all murder and cover-ups though—there was a lot of joy in it too.

Namely in the form of Tommasso Capelli.

Tommy stayed with Dash for a solid week, several days after his apartment was cleared of being a crime scene. When Tommy was finally ready to head back to his place, he invited Dash with him. They spent almost every night together, even when their jobs pulled them away, and Dash loved having someone to go home to.

There was nothing better after a stressful cleaning job than to fall into bed with Tommy and get a nice, sleepy back rub.

Though it was still too early to say for certain, Dash was confident that he and Tommy had quite a bright future ahead of them. It was everything he could have ever wanted and more, and he was happy. Tommy was kind, funny, a fantastic cook, and absolutely *phenomenal* in the sack.

Okay, not that the sex was really *that* important, and Dash had continued to stay clear of that giant dick ring, but it was still damn good.

Dash had just come home from a long and blistering day at the crematory, and he headed right to the shower. He'd had a cleaning job last night, a relatively simple problem at 42 West Hill Street. It was only one body, but it had been up on the second floor and the numerous bullet holes did not make it any lighter.

He was very grateful for the hot water to rinse away the funk of the day and ease his sore back.

Tommy was coming over for dinner, and Dash was going to cook for them. Well, he was going to *try* and cook, no doubt under Tommy's strict supervision, and hope that whatever they ended up with was edible.

Worst case scenario, they could just order out.

Dash stepped out of the bathroom with a towel on, startled when he saw Tommy lounging across his bed. "What the fuck!"

"Hi, babe." Tommy grinned. "Surprise?"

"Uh, yeah, a little bit." Dash laughed. "You're not supposed to be here for another hour." He walked to the bed, leaning down for a kiss.

"Mm, I got bored." Tommy reached for Dash's towel. "I missed you."

Dash tugged his towel out of Tommy's hand. "Easy now."

"But I *missed* you." Tommy's smile grew sly.

"Yes, and we're gonna cook dinner first—"

"Why does dinner have to be first? Why can't we

come and then have dinner?" Tommy grabbed Dash's hips.

"Will you quit it?" Dash laughed as Tommy dragged him down into bed with him, and he struggled to keep his towel on. "Come on! I gotta get dressed!"

"No. In fact, no, you don't." Tommy easily pinned Dash and smooched along his neck. "We're grown-ups. We don't have to wear clothes."

"Only one of us acts like a damn grown-up and it's not you!" Dash squirmed.

"I'm super grown-up!" Tommy wiggled between Dash's thighs. "I'm so mature, mm, and very, very adult."

"How many video game systems do you own again?"

"Shush."

"And how often do we watch cartoons?"

"Hey, *Archer* is definitely not meant for kids. Now be quiet, I'm trying to do somethin' here." Tommy dragged his mouth down Dash's chest.

"And what exactly is that?" Dash asked, even though he already knew.

"Insert my penis into your gorgeous body repeatedly until we've both reached climax?"

"But dinner..." Dash gave one final protest, although it was pretty weak considering how hard he was beneath his towel.

"Dinner will be delicious and wonderful...." Tommy unwrapped Dash's towel. "After I'm done with you."

Dash stared down at Tommy between his naked thighs and sighed as if very annoyed. "Okay, fine. Go ahead. Have your wicked way with me."

"Thank you, I will." Tommy winked and then took Dash's cock into his mouth.

Dash dropped his head back into the pillows with a sharp groan, panting already as Tommy sucked him expertly. The wet suction and the hot friction of Tommy's tongue was perfect, and Tommy's fingers squeezed his balls with just the right amount of pressure to make his breath catch.

Tommy was always so good at this, especially at bringing Dash right to the edge and teasing him mercilessly. He'd take his time, make this last for hours sometimes, though his fingers already probing at Dash's hole betrayed an eagerness to move things along faster this evening.

That was fine by Dash.

He grabbed the lube from the bedside table drawer, popped open the cap, and slicked up his fingers. He reached around his hip to get to his asshole, pushing Tommy's fingers out of his way to replace them with his own. He arched his hips and spread his legs, pushing inside of himself despite the awkward angle.

"There you go," Tommy urged, lavishing Dash's cock with long licks. "Fuck, there you go, baby. Get yourself ready for me."

Dash couldn't press deep enough to open himself up, and he whined, struggling to go farther than the mere tips of his fingers. "Fuck, I'm trying."

Tommy's hand returned, sliding through the lube and quickly taking back over. He slid his finger in as he sucked Dash's cock into his mouth once more, bobbing his head in the same gentle rhythm as his plunging finger.

The combined sensations were electric, and Dash rocked down in search of even more friction. He wiped his fingers off on the towel beneath him before digging into Tommy's hair, groaning happily. "There we go, baby. There, just like that. F-fuck! Yes!"

Tommy swallowed Dash's dick effortlessly, and every thrust of his finger drove Dash closer to the edge. He gasped when Tommy added a second, and he was ready for the full stretch of Tommy's cock inside of him now.

Dash bucked his hips more purposefully, but Tommy seemed content to keep deep throating him. He met Tommy's eyes, and he said bluntly, "Will you come on and fuck me already?"

"Mm?" Tommy hummed around his mouthful, and he gave a playful thrust of his fingers.

"Tommy!"

Tommy pulled off. "What is it, baby?"

"Come on." Dash tried urging Tommy up his body. "Will you get your fine ass up here?"

"I'm very busy at the moment," Tommy replied as his fingers continued to push inside of Dash. "I'll be right with you."

Dash glared, his brain scrambling for a way to convince Tommy. If he actually had a maid uniform laying around, it would be easy. When Tommy got in these teasing moods of his, it was difficult to get him moving along to the main event.

But there was one thing...

Dash licked his lips and said, "You can fuck me with your dick ring in."

That got Tommy's attention, and he blinked at Dash in surprise. "Really? You wanna try it?"

"Yes. I don't care how your dick gets in me right now as long as it's in me." Dash smirked as Tommy's jaw dropped. "So, is that a yes?"

Tommy didn't reply at first as he was too busy flailing around the bed, trying to remove his clothes. One of his shoes hit the bedside table in his feverish divestment, and then he kneeled between Dash's legs, his hair ruffled and his face flushed. "Oh, it's a big yes."

"Yeah?" Dash smiled.

"For fuckin' sure, but you tell me if it's too much, all right?" Tommy picked up the lube. "Only takes two seconds to take it out, you know."

"I know." Dash watched Tommy lubing himself up, and he felt a quick ping of nerves.

Damn, that ring was huge.

"So, like this?" Dash asked. "Or, uh, a different position?"

"How about on your side?" Tommy suggested.

"Okay." Dash rolled over, drawing his legs up toward his chest. "Like this?"

"That's perfect, baby." Tommy lay down behind him, curling against his back. He kissed Dash's shoulder. "We're gonna go nice and slow, okay? And you just tell me if you want me to take it out."

"But you like it, right?" Dash glanced back. "It feels better when you have it in?"

"Baby." Tommy smiled warmly. "I don't care how I'm

with you as long as I'm with you. Yes, my dick ring feels good, but it's no fun if you're not diggin' it too."

"Okay." Dash took a deep breath. "Go ahead."

"I got you." Tommy nuzzled Dash's neck. "Nice and easy..."

Dash flinched when he first felt the metal of the ring. It was smooth and unrelenting, an odd contrast to the tender firmness of Tommy's cock. The first push was strange because he was immediately aware of the jewelry, and it didn't feel like it belonged there.

It was rubbing against his most intimate places, and he was surprised by how it sort of tickled. The sensation was enough to distract him from the velvety slide of Tommy's cock thrusting in and out of his body, though not entirely uncomfortable. It wasn't exactly pleasurable either though, and Dash tried shifting his hips, hoping that it would change.

Tommy squeezed Dash's hip. "Doing okay?"

"Yeah. Feels funny." Dash wiggled.

"Almost in, baby." Tommy smooched Dash's shoulder again, rocking forward in steady thrusts. "Mm, feelin' good?"

"Just keep going," Dash urged as he tried to find a better position. He drew one of his knees to his chest and then tilted so he was almost on his face, breathing through the stretch of Tommy's cock pushing deeper inside of him. Tommy moved with him so he was practically on top of him now, still thrusting away with gentle strokes, and Dash gasped at a bolt of unexpected pleasure.

Tommy's cock ring rubbed right against Dash's

prostate as he withdrew, and it hit it again when he slipped back in.

The pressure was brief but insistent, but it still made Dash shiver.

"Good?" Tommy asked. "You okay, baby?"

"Yeah, mm, it... it felt really good for a second." Dash took a deep breath.

"You mean... here?" Tommy pulled his cock out halfway so he could focus the jewelry right there in that same magical spot by thrusting in short bursts.

"Mmm, yup, yup, right there!" Dash groaned low, and he arched up to increase the friction. The ring was rubbing back and forth over that bundle of nerves with exact precision, and it felt amazing. He missed the depth of having Tommy's full cock fuck him properly, but this was incredible too.

"There, baby?" Tommy mouthed at Dash's ear, squeezing his hip.

"Yes, f-fuck!" Dash moaned breathlessly. "God, that feels nice..."

"Want some more, baby?"

"Yeah, come on." Dash rolled so he was on his stomach, his legs spreading. "More. I want more. Right now."

"Mmm, I love when you get all bossy." Tommy chuckled as he readjusted himself, pressing against Dash's back. He thrust forward, burying his cock deep inside of Dash's hole. "God, there it is. Fuck, yeah."

Dash grunted, breathing through the powerful ache of Tommy's cock in this position. The jewelry was still impossible to ignore, but he was starting to like how it felt as Tommy moved.

Tommy fucked him slow and hard, and then he'd pull out just enough to rub the ring back into his prostate. He'd fuck him again, slowly building the rhythm, over and over until Dash was ready to lose his mind.

The exciting stimulation plus the drag of the ring with Tommy's thick cock was intense, and Dash moaned for more. He let out a loud shout when Tommy really started giving it to him, fucking him hard and fast, and the building heat was fantastic. Tommy's cock felt heavy, hot, and Dash squeezed around him just to increase the sensation.

He loved how Tommy touched him, and the filthy things he whispered in his ear sent shivers down his spine.

"God, you feel so fuckin' good. I can't wait to come in you, baby. I love filling up your sweet little ass." Tommy groaned eagerly. "Nothin' feels as good as you, fuckin' nothin', fuck! Nobody takes my cock like you do. I'm gonna keep on fuckin' you until you're fuckin' drippin', baby."

"Come on," Dash said with a grunt. "Come on, baby. Give it to me. Fuckin' do it!"

Tommy slid his arm beneath Dash's chest, reaching up to grab his shoulder so he could pull him into each fierce slam. "Yeah, you want it? You want my fuckin' come, baby?"

"Yes! Fuck!" Dash could hardly speak as the force of Tommy's pounding was taking his breath away. The pressure was building faster and faster, and waves of pleasure were washing over him and drowning his senses. He cried out when Tommy's cock swelled inside of him, and his hole flooded with a hot load of come.

"God, yes!" Tommy grunted, slamming in hard. "There we go, there we go, baby."

"Mmm, fuck, that's good." Dash closed his eyes, savoring the warmth and the new slippery slide Tommy's come added to his thrusting. "Fuck..."

"Come here, baby." Tommy was rolling back onto his side, urging Dash to move with him.

Dash gasped as Tommy grabbed his cock, stroking him fast. "Mm, yes!" He arched back, grinding on Tommy's cock still buried inside of him. He focused on the tight grip of Tommy's hand, panting as he felt himself drifting over that delicious edge of climax. "Almost... almost... f-fuck..."

"Come on, baby," Tommy urged, giving Dash a few hard thrusts. "Get it for me, baby."

"I'm... mmm, fuck. Keep fucking me, keep fucking me!"

"Come for me, baby!" Tommy fucked Dash fast, jerking him off in time with the quick snap of his hips.

Dash gasped, his thighs tensed, and the heat in his loins was boiling over. "Mmm, there, there! Fuck! I'm coming, I'm coming!" He groaned as his cock pulsed across the bed, and he went limp in Tommy's arms, submitting to his frantic thrusts and his sure grip. "Mm, fuck, yes!"

"There you go, there it is..." Tommy smothered Dash's shoulder and the back of his neck with kisses, slowly drawing his slams to a halt. He let go of Dash's cock after one last squeeze, and he hugged his waist. "Mmmph. Damn."

"Uh-huh. Damn." Dash laughed.

"Aren't you glad we had sex first?"

"Mm. Very glad." Dash looked back at Tommy. "Except now we gotta clean up and instead of taking a nap, I have to go cook."

"We both know I'm going to end up cooking, so it's totally fine."

"Asshole!"

"What?" Tommy grinned. "Just saying, we know what happens when you cook. There's fire, explosions, people start screaming..."

"Ha ha, very funny." Dash snorted, shifting forward so Tommy's wilting cock withdrew. He made a face as the ring caught on its way out, and he said, "Okay, and yes, the dick ring was a delight and all, but maybe not an all the time thing?"

"Ah, got it. So, special days like anniversaries, Christmas, Halloween?"

"You're already thinking about Halloween?"

"Hell yeah, I am." Tommy dragged Dash in for a kiss. "Mm, I already know what I'm going to dress up as. You too."

"If you say a maid—"

"No, no, no. There's been a change of plans. *I'm* going to be the maid, and you're going to be an accountant."

Dash laughed, and he ran his hand over Tommy's cheek. "An accountant, huh? And how exactly do I dress up as an accountant?"

"Fuck if I know. Put a big calculator in your pocket or something." Tommy smirked.

"You think we're still gonna be together at Halloween?"

"Duh." Tommy kissed him, and he let it linger for a long moment. "Kinda planning on being with you forever."

Dash's heart promptly stuttered, and he couldn't believe Tommy was being so sweet. Then again, it was only a matter of time before he said—

"Or however long it takes to get your fine ass in a maid skirt," Tommy went on. "You know, whatever comes first. Maid outfit, forever, so many choices here."

Ah, there it was.

Dash chuckled, and he kissed Tommy's forehead. "Come on. Let's get cleaned up so I can go destroy my kitchen making dinner for us."

"Hey, you didn't say no that time."

Dash smirked. "It wasn't a yes."

"But it wasn't a no." Tommy grinned. "Just so we're clear, even if you wear the maid outfit, I'm still bettin' on forever."

"Forever is a good start," Dash agreed. "I think I can work with that."

"Good." Tommy nuzzled their noses together before pressing a sweet kiss to Dash's lips. "Mmm, unless..."

"Unless what?"

"Unless something awful happens, like I die of food poisoning before then—"

"Shut up, accountant."

"Shutting up." Tommy cleared his throat. "Oh, but wait, one last thing."

"What?"

"My uncle's been real busy doin' all this stuff with the family and making sure our businesses are all on track." Tommy fidgeted. "So, he hasn't had a lot of free time to handle everything that needs handling, you know?"

He actually looked nervous, which immediately put Dash on alert. "Like what?"

"Like takin' care of my grandpa's ashes. My dad's too."

"Do you need some help with... an urn?" Dash didn't understand what Tommy was trying to say. "Casting a stepping stone or something?"

"He wants me to go to Italy," Tommy replied, "and I want you to come with me."

"Say what?"

"He wants me to go to Italy, and I want you to come with me," Tommy repeated. "It would just be for a few days. I know we both got our business shit to attend to and you'll have to figure out shit with your cleaning, but uh, yeah. I've never been, you know, and I thought it could be a fun lil' vacation for us."

"Wow." Dash grinned. "Yes! I would love to."

"Hell yeah!" Tommy smooched Dash and hugged him close. "I can't fuckin' wait. It's gonna be amazing. We're gonna spread their ashes, say a few words, and then see everything Italy has to fuckin' offer."

"You know it's probably illegal to spread ashes at that winery, right?"

"That'll just make it more fun."

"Right, because it can't be fun if it's not a little bad?"

"Just a little."

They shared a few more kisses before necessity drew them out of bed to get cleaned up. Tommy followed Dash into the kitchen so they could get dinner started, and Dash's many valiant attempts to make gnocchi from scratch went south quickly. Tommy was happy to help with only minimal teasing, and the rest of the meal was a fantastic success.

Dash could definitely see a future with Tommy. He couldn't wait for their next big adventure together, although hopefully there wouldn't be any murders or bullets flying around. He'd never been so thankful that he'd taken a chance on that mysterious letter and visited the private club at the Menagerie Hotel.

He hadn't known exactly what he was looking for when he first went there—some work, maybe someone to burn some steam off with and have some fun. What he ended up finding, however, was all that and more.

Dash had found something special with Tommy, a relationship where he could finally be himself, totally and honestly. It was the sort of connection worth fighting for, and he was never going to let anything get in the way of the bright future they had ahead of them.

God help anyone who tried.

KEEP READING

Check out all the fantastic titles in The Elite series. All books can be read as standalones and in any order. They are connected only through a shared premise.

ABOUT THE AUTHOR

K.L. "Kat" Hiers is an embalmer, restorative artist, and queer writer. Licensed in both funeral directing and funeral service, they worked in the death industry for nearly a decade. Their first love was always telling stories, and they have been writing for over twenty years, penning their very first book at just eight years old. Publishers generally do not accept manuscripts in Hello Kitty notebooks, however, but they never gave up.

Following the success of their first novel, *Cold Hard Cash*, they now enjoy writing professionally, focusing on spinning tales of sultry passion, exotic worlds, and emotional journeys. They love attending horror movie conventions and indulging in cosplay of their favorite characters. They live in Zebulon, NC, with their family, including their children, some of whom have paws and a few that only pretend to because they think it's cute.

https://www.klhiers.com

ALSO BY K. L. HIERS

COLD HARD CASH

COLD HARD CASH ON AUDIOBOOK

SUCKER FOR LOVE MYSTERIES

SUCKER FOR LOVE ON AUDIOBOOK

Acsquidentally In Love

DAYS OF MONSTERS

13 Days of Monster F#cking: Volume 1

13 Days of Monster F#cking: Volume 2

8 Days of Monstrous Pride

38469642R00106